C000007805

# SHADOW SONG

## THE EVERLASTING CHRONICLES

## K.G. REUSS

BOOK 2

The Everlasting Chronicles: Shadow Song

© 2018 by K.G. Reuss. All rights reserved.

No part of this book may be reproduced in any written, electronic, recording, or photocopying without written permission of the publisher or author. The exception would be in the case of brief quotations embodied in the critical articles or reviews and pages where permission is specifically granted by the author.

This book is a work of fiction. Names, characters, places, and incidents either are products of the author's overactive imagination or are used fictitiously. Any resemblance to actual persons, living or dead, or events is entirely coincidental.

Signed Books may be purchased by contacting the author at:

www.Facebook.com/kgreuss

Cover Design: Covers by Christian

Publisher: Amazon Direct, Books From Beyond

Editor: N-D-Scribable Services

First Edition

*"It is better to be feared than loved, if you cannot be both* -Niccolo Machiavelli.

*For Dusty.*
*They're real. They exist. I told you so.*

# PROLOGUE

*I* had a firm belief that we shouldn't speak ill of the dead. They were gone, leaving behind only their memories. They had no way to defend themselves against harsh words or brutal truths. What was done was done. Let them rest in peace.

All my thoughts on that were flung out of the highest window from the tallest tower the moment the beautiful, green-eyed, raven-haired, ivory-skinned angel entered my life. I didn't know at the time that she was going to change my world forever. *How could I?* I was four, and she was only three.

One moment I was in my room, lying in bed after my mother had tucked me in, and the next there was this terrible pull in my gut. It took me from my room and left me frightened in a dark place filled with growls, snarls, and voices hissing through the surrounding blackness. It was my time in shadow. My first time through the darkest places of the Veil. Back then, I didn't know it was called the Veil.

I cried. I remembered that. I didn't know where I was or why I was there. I could hear the voices around me. I could feel their claws on my skin. So, I ran. I ran as far and as fast as my little legs could take me.

Suddenly, there was a light — a beautiful, promising light spilling through an opening. As I ran closer, I could make out the form of a girl sitting on the floor of a room. Her blanket was wrapped tightly around her as she rocked back and forth. I burst into the light as the claws scraped my legs, arms, and neck, and tumbled into the girl's bedroom through her closet door.

She didn't pay any attention to me. Confused about why she wasn't seeing me, I looked down and saw that I was as black as night, having turned into a shadow myself. My heart hammered like mad in my chest. While I was afraid for myself, I was even more scared for her. She continued to rock, her green eyes wavering as she stared at her bedroom door. Still frightened about what had just happened to me, and how I'd gotten there, I backed into the corner to watch her. I wanted to talk to her but couldn't. I didn't have the right words to say, and she already looked frightened enough. Yelling from somewhere else in the house floated to me, the screams getting louder. She rocked faster as heavy footsteps thudded down the hall.

"You will *not* touch her!" a woman screamed. "*Por favor!*"

My fear for the girl grew as the door to her room slammed open. The girl gave a start, her eyes wider as the menacing form of a large, hulking man entered her room, his green eyes wild.

"Everly," he growled, stomping into the room. She scooted away from him, her small hands still clutching her blanket and a small stuffed rabbit. "They want you."

"Don't touch her!" the woman shrieked, rushing into the room. She looked like the girl—long dark hair and a pretty face. But her eyes were chocolate brown where the girl's were emerald green. The man reached out and struck the woman across the face, sending her flying into the wall where she banged her head and slid down, her body limp.

"Mommy!" little Everly cried out, scrambling to her feet. The little girl tried to run behind her bed, but the man was fast and caught her by her hair then yanked her back to him. He gripped her tightly. His hand clasped over her mouth as she kicked and screamed.

"It's started! They want you! You're a curse they can have!"

2

He tugged her small struggling body to the closet I'd just escaped from and opened the door. The wails from the monsters inside caused me to cover my ears. I watched in horror as many sets of gnarled, dead hands reached out. The stench of death permeated the room. The girl was thrust forward and captured by the creatures in her closet.

"Daddy! Daddy! Please!" she screamed as they tore at her, dragging her into the darkness. He only stood there watching with a grim expression on his face as she was taken away.

Her father had let her go. I watched as he went to his wife who lay unconscious on the floor. He scooped her limp body up easily and left the room. Turning, I stared at the closed closet door, my mind made up before I even realized it.

I drew in a deep breath as I approached the door. I was going to save her. It was a decision easily made. I was put there for a reason.

*She* was my reason, and I'd die before I let something happen to her.

# CHAPTER 1

"*A*re we *really* doing this?" Eric groaned, rubbing his blue eyes, his messy blond hair falling across his forehead. "I hate doing these raids. I'm exhausted for days after."

"You wouldn't be if you let Brandon or me heal you," I pointed out as I pulled my sword out and examined it. The titanium silver gleamed beneath the overhead lights of our weapons room.

"Brandon has a hard-enough time keeping up with all the healing he has to do with Damien," Eric argued, looking over to Damien, the dark-haired shifter who was eating a bag of potato chips instead of making sure his weapons were in order for the night's raid on a carrion nest.

"Are you complaining again, Craft?" Damien asked, finally getting up from the table he was sitting on, tossing his now empty bag of chips into the trash and wiping his hands on his pant legs.

"Just about you," Eric retorted.

"If you two would put as much effort into getting your things together as you do in antagonizing one another, we'd already be halfway through this raid," I mumbled irritably, stuffing the blade into the sheath on my back before grabbing two daggers and strapping them to my legs beneath my long, black cloak. "Brandon and Adam are already done and ready to go."

"Like you have anything to be worried about," Eric grunted, stuffing his dagger into the strap on his leg. "You're just going to charge in there, kill some carrion, and walk out without a scratch."

"Probably," I shrugged, knowing he was more than likely right. I *never* got hurt. Because I was very good at my job. I scooped up my favorite set of throwing knifes and attached them to the holster on my chest. I paused as a strange warmness washed over me. It traveled from my head all the way to my toes making me adjust my shirt collar. My whole body felt tingly and light, almost like that moment right before sleep claimed me each night.

"What the hell?" I murmured, trying to shake it off. It was just anticipation for the evening's impending ordeal. That was all. It disappeared a moment later leaving me feeling lightheaded and woozy. I swallowed down the nausea and drew in a deep, calming breath as I pushed my silver hair away from my damp forehead.

*I'm stressed out over the Cipher threat. I'm overworked and exhausted. That's all. It's nothing. Damn Cipher.* With them being in direct opposition to the Order, it fell to me and my crew to eliminate as many of them as possible. I made a mental note to get a decent night's sleep since it had been weeks since I'd actually had one. The nagging familiarity that had accompanied the tingly was still gnawing at me though.

"You know what I can't wait for?" Eric continued as he eyed his blade.

"What?" I asked, still frowning as I tried to push my troubled thoughts away.

"The day you get paired off after an induction. Adam got Chloe last go. Brandon got Amanda. I can only imagine how it would change you," Eric mused, a tiny smirk on his lips. He was referring to our pairing ceremony in Conexus where we stood on a dais and let our blood decide who our best suited partner would be. And it wasn't a *love* thing. It was a fighting thing. Anyone could get paired with anyone else. I hadn't been paired. *Ever.* I didn't figure I ever would be.

It would have to be a crazy strong Special to be able to match up with me. But if I ever found one, my abilities would be out of this world strong—and so would theirs. It would bring a whole new level of badassery to our group.

"That won't happen. I'm a machine all on my own." I shot a half-assed grin at him, still feeling weird inside, that damn nagging familiarity getting stronger.

"Well, Mr. Machine. We going to get some breakfast after we finish this shit?" Damien asked, surveying one of his blades carefully before glancing over his shoulder at me. "Because I'm already hungry."

"You just ate an entire bag of chips, *and* I'm pretty sure Sloane is going to kill you when she sees you drank all the milk. Again." Eric rolled his eyes at the hulking shifter.

"She'll have to touch me to do that." Damien waggled his eyebrows at Eric who shook his head, smiling.

"Sloane doesn't have to touch you. She could probably end your life from twenty feet away all while tying her shoes," I commented, mentioning the powerful caster in our ranks and one of our roommates. "And I'll be surprised if she doesn't. At the very least, she's going to get on your case. Hard. You know how she is about empty milk cartons in the fridge."

"I know." Damien grinned wider. "Why do you think I leave them there?"

"You're a glutton for punishment." Eric slapped Damien on the back, and the two exchanged laughs.

I doubled over suddenly, my head spinning wildly as the warmness from before became an intense heat.

"Shadow?" Eric asked, concerned. Damien snapped his head up and looked at me.

"You OK, man?" Damien asked, stepping toward me, the worry evident in his now serious voice. I was never sick. And Damien was never serious. Something was very wrong.

"I-I'm not feeling well," I murmured, reaching out to steady myself. I found my two best friends at my side, trying to keep me on my feet.

7

"Get him a chair," Eric commanded tightly. A moment later Damien was sliding a chair beneath me. I sat back on it still feeling woozy.

"Man, you're pale," Damien commented. "Can you heal?"

I frowned as I tested my healing. Nothing happened. If anything, it made me feel sicker. I shook my head weakly, leaning forward with my head in my hands. I tugged at my silvery locks in frustration as my vision blurred.

"Go get Brandon," Eric commanded. Damien was out of the room and back within seconds with Brandon, our Fae healer, in tow.

"Shadow, what's going on?" Brandon asked, kneeling in front of me. I managed to raise my head to look at him and swayed to the side, an intense pulling starting in my core. I felt like I was being torn in two. It was a feeling similar to the one I got when I shadow melded— one of my many gifts, gifts that I could bestow on my crew in Conexus.

"Shit," I moaned. Brandon's hands came out, and he placed them on either side of my head. His eyes closed as he tried to heal me.

"It's not working," he muttered as he shook his messy dark curls in frustration. "I-I don't understand. It should work."

I fell forward then, knocking Brandon roughly aside and hit the ground with a painful *thud.* I managed to roll over with a groan, my eyes focused on the overhead light. There was a scurry of activity as my friends bustled around, trying to help me.

"Shadow? Shadow!" Damien called out. He shook me, but I couldn't rip myself away from whatever was beginning to happen to me. It was so strong, it left me helpless.

"What the hell!" Eric shouted frantically. "Man, what's going on? Shadow! Come on! Brandon, help me get him to the couch! Damien, call Brighton. Get him here quick. See if Madam Ann is around, too."

I was lifted into the air and moved to the couch in the commons room, my body unable to move on its own. Beyond my eyes were flashes of places I hadn't seen in years as I stared at the ceiling, unable to move my body. My friends' voices clamored in the background still, but *this* trumped everything, even Brandon's efforts to bring me back again.

*Her* face flashed in my mind, a blur of dark hair and beautiful emerald colored eyes. I hadn't seen her since we were twelve. The girl I'd once cared deeply for but now hated with every fiber of my being. My mind raced through the last time I'd ever seen her. I'd been pulled to her ever since I was four years old. She'd been a tiny, terrified three-year-old at the time of our first encounter. In all the years I'd been drawn to her, I'd only spoken to her once. Not because I didn't want to, but because I was afraid to. I didn't want to frighten her. She was already a troubled girl having to deal with her abusive father. And *them*. The dead.

*"Daddy! No! Please!" she shouted in her tiny voice, kicking and screaming. I could hear her as I raced through the shadows, my mind in overdrive.*

*Panic surged through me. I wasn't going to get to her fast enough. Her father might actually win this time.*

*With a thud, I landed in her bedroom as I'd skipped through the shadows to get to her. But she wasn't there. A crash came from downstairs, making me take the stairs as fast as I could. I burst into her living room and found her bound with her father tying a gag tightly around her mouth. Without thinking twice, the large man lifted her small body up and pushed her into the coat closet.*

*"Let them have you if they want you!" he bellowed, slamming the door closed on her. I rushed forward and threw myself through the door, my form a shadow which was naked to the Nattie eye, people who didn't possess powers like me. And even those who did, wouldn't see me. I'd always been good at walking and existing with the shadows, hence my name.*

*The inside of the closet was gone. Instead, it was a void of shadow. A place where the darkest creatures existed in torment. I'd been there many times. I ran forward, letting the attraction to her guide me. And then, there she was.*

*She lay curled in a tiny ball as the creatures of shadow—the wraiths and the lost ones, souls who wandered—tore at her ferociously, cackling wickedly. I didn't hesitate. I plunged my blade through every single one of them until there was nothing left but her coiled tightly in a dirty, white nightgown.*

9

*Rolling her over, I took the gag out of her mouth. Her eyes were closed, and her face bled from their nails scratching her. I tried to heal her, but my powers didn't work in the void. I lifted her limp body in my arms and carried her to the exit, wanting to get out of there as soon as possible. Even at twelve, I was a tall, muscular guy. Muffled shouting filtered through from the other side of the closet door as we approached it.*

*Her mom was home. She'd help.*

*"Everly?" I called out, cutting the ropes off her wrists and ankles as I laid her near the door. "Everly? It's me. It's Shadow. Please wake up. Please?" I begged, clinging to her. With trembling fingers, I pushed her damp hair away from her face, and her eyelids fluttered before opening. I was greeted with her pretty green eyes gazing up at me.*

*"You came," she murmured, her small hand reaching out for me. Her fingers brushed my cheek, causing me to close my eyes at her tender touch. I pulled her into my arms again, hating being away from her even for a second. A moment later, her eyelids trembled, and she went unconscious, her body once again limp in my arms. She'd probably never remember this moment.*

*The doorknob rattled loudly, and I looked down at Everly. My Everly. Her mom was going to help her. As much as it hurt me to do, I laid her down on the closet floor and stepped back into the shadows, my sword once again gripped tightly in my hands. A moment later, the door was jerked open, and Mrs. Torres let out a cry as she dragged Everly into her arms. Voices clamored behind her as police entered the house. Beyond Mrs. Torres Everly's father was crumpled on the floor, a broken vase at his head. She'd knocked him out cold. A sense of satisfaction washed over me. I knew it was the end for Mr. Torres, and his reign of terror over my Everly.*

I didn't see her again after that. The attraction disappeared. She disappeared. It could've been from my new hatred of her that she couldn't reach me any longer. Or maybe she just stopped needing me. It was right after I saved her that I went home to find my mother dead. All because I hadn't been there to keep her safe.

I was left heartbroken, the two people who mattered most to me in the world, gone —one I had to learn to let go of and one I began to hate. I threw myself into learning my abilities, into doing everything my father and the Order commanded of me. Because I'd promised myself I would find her again, and she'd pay for being the reason I wasn't home to protect my mother from the vamp who took her life.

The heat finally waned. My body twitched. My eyes moved. And I was able to breathe deeply again. I flexed my fingers, blinking my eyes. Even when I was a kid, *that* never happened to me. It was similar but definitely not the same.

I sat up tiredly as Eric and Brandon backed away.

"You OK?" Brandon asked uncertainly.

"I think so," I murmured, rubbing my thighs briskly before getting to my feet. I was still tipsy, and Eric jumped to my side as I swayed. "I'm good."

"You don't look so good," Eric commented, moving away from me so I could have some space. I didn't reply because Damien and Headmaster Brighton entered the commons.

"What happened?" Brighton demanded, his gray eyes sweeping over me quickly.

"I'm not sure," I replied, sitting back down on the couch. Brandon thrust a glass of water in my hand, and I thanked him quickly. "I just felt weird there for a minute."

"Has it ever happened before?" Brighton asked, coming to survey me quickly.

"No. Not like that." I shook my head. Brighton paused and looked me in the eye.

"So, it's happened before?"

"*Not* like that," I repeated evenly, my eyes locked on his. He glanced at the guys in the room before peering back to me and giving me a tight nod. He knew me well enough to know that I wasn't one to share too much information, so pressing me on it wasn't a good idea.

"And now? How are you feeling?" Brighton asked delicately, a frown on his tired face. He reached out and tilted my head up. A small light in his hand flashed quickly in my eyes as he surveyed me. Seemingly satisfied, he backed away and waited for me to answer.

"Like I could run a marathon—twice," I answered honestly. It felt as if nothing had happened to me.

"It was probably just an episode of nerves. You guys are headed into a big nest tonight, right?" Brighton asked. He knew damn well it wasn't nerves. We all did, but no one said that. Instead, we all agreed.

"Right. Well, I don't think it's anything serious. For now." He gave me a stern look. "But do come get me if anything changes. Madam Ann is out in Easterly, the Fae realm, visiting family still so she won't be available."

"No problem." I gave Brighton a curt nod. He eyed me once more before departing with a disapproving sigh. Brighton, our overseer in Conexus, was a good guy. Damien liked to refer to him as our glorified babysitter, a remark that often left Brighton threatening Damien with detention. Brighton's job was to make sure we did what we were meant to do which was to protect. Brighton and I had an unspoken, respectful bond with one another. He recognized that I ran the school more than he did. We both knew our place within our world and didn't bother to fight about it.

"Are we even still going?" Damien cleared his throat, breaking the awkward silence.

"Yes," I answered without hesitation. I wasn't about to sacrifice getting into one of the Cipher nests just because I had an unsteady, strange moment. I'd rather pass out and wake up surrounded by the blood-sucking leeches I loathed with my entire being, than call off a hunt just because I felt *odd*. Vampires were the worst of the worst.

"Man, that was messed up. I don't know if it's a good idea—" Eric started, but I shook my head, silencing him.

"This is our *job*. We have intel that the Cipher have a nest nearby. We'd be fools to let it go simply because I had a moment. We have a duty to remove the threat. And we will," I said determinedly, my voice taking on the authoritative tone I used when I had to get tough with my crew. The Cipher had every type of being we had and then some. We were a little more discriminating about who we allowed within our ranks.

"Damn," Damien muttered. "I really wanted to be here when Sloane found the empty milk carton."

"Don't worry. I'm sure we'll hear about it when we get back," I chuckled softly, still feeling odd. I shook it off. It couldn't be her. Everly was gone. I hoped she stayed that way, too. I wasn't sure what I'd do if I saw her again.

But something deep within me hoped that maybe, just maybe, she was out there thinking of me too.

# CHAPTER 2

"On your left!" I shouted at Eric as a carrion lurched forward with its pitch-black eyes and lolling mouth both opened wide as it lunged forward. Eric swept his sword down and cut through the beast, leaving it to fall to the ground at his feet, dead.

"Shadow! Behind you!" Damien called out. I whipped around and slashed through another carrion while throwing my dagger and nailing another one in the chest. I'd taken out at least twenty of the foul, magic-leeching creatures—beings who were once casters but had screwed themselves by overindulging in the dark arts. Now, they roamed around, starving for more magic, needing the very thing that had overcome them and sucked the sense from their bodies. They were servants to a darker power now, and there was no coming back from that.

We hacked and slashed our way through the nest. Adam, our resident warlock, wiped at his brow and shook his head.

"This is ridiculous! When did it get so bad?" he growled, his dark hair wet with sweat and his lips turned down into a frown. "Why are there so many of them?"

"Good question," I muttered. There did seem to be a lot more than usual. Our intel indicated that the Cipher had many of the forsaken and other dark creatures and beasts under their control, but this seemed like a lot, even for them.

"It's like they're gathering an army," Eric commented. "I mean, they always have been, but this?" He gestured around to the bodies strewn on the ground. "This is a bit much. We had to have taken out at least a hundred carrion tonight."

"Yeah, another night, another heap of dead crap. Can we get food now?" Damien yawned widely. Brandon chuckled and stuffed his blade back into his black cloak. We all followed suit. Damien had a point. We'd worked up an appetite.

"Adam, burn the bodies," I commanded, nodding to the dead carrion. He obliged with a nod. Instantly his hands erupted into brilliant blue flames, then the bodies ignited. They sizzled and crackled for a brief second before only dust remained, leaving just the ugly stench of ash hanging in the air.

"You do realize it's only after midnight, right?" I chuckled as we walked away and entered a dark alley, morphing from our shadow selves into our real selves—all of us in long, dark cloaks and all-black hunting attire.

"That's AM, my friend," Damien countered. "Which means morning, and what do you eat in the morning? Breakfast. I'm thinking waffles."

We were sharing a laugh when I suddenly fell to my knees, clutching my chest. The heat was back, and this time it brought an intense pain with it.

"Shadow?" Eric called out, rushing to my side.

"What's going on?" Adam asked, frowning down at me as I tried to breathe. Each movement of air only created more agony in my chest.

"Is it the same as earlier?" Brandon demanded, his hands automatically going to the sides of my head. I felt him try to heal me, but it couldn't flow past whatever block was happening. He growled in frustration and tried again.

"Dude, what the hell, man?" Damien shouted. "Let's get him out of here. We need to get him to Brighton. Eric, get on the other side and help me carry him—"

He didn't get to finish his sentence, or maybe he did, and I just didn't hear it. Before any of us realized what was happening, the tug in my core grew, and I was pulled into shadow, disappearing and leaving them behind.

*I* t wasn't like when I was a kid. I soared through it and landed with a thump on a hallway floor. The pain and strangeness I'd been feeling disappeared, and I swallowed hard as I got to my feet and examined my surroundings. I didn't recognize the place at all. In front of me was a closed door. A shiver traveled up my spine. There was *something* behind that door that I didn't want to see. I knew it, but the desire to open the damn thing was eating at me. Just as I was reaching out for it, the door was flung open. I quickly pressed my shadowed body to the wall beside it.

A girl with wild green eyes rushed out of the room in tiny, pink shorts and a tank top. Her hair was a long, dark tangled mess flying behind her. She dashed down the hallway, her small body quaking with fear. With haste, she threw open another door and disappeared inside without a backward glance.

I stood staring in the direction she'd gone, stunned. *Everly.* It was her. I knew it without a doubt. I'd never forget those green eyes. And she needed me, or I wouldn't be there. I let out a low growl, not knowing what was driving me other than my sheer hatred for the girl. Rivaling the anger I'd harbored towards her for the past five years was an overwhelming ache in my heart that I forced away. Drawing my blade out of my cloak, I stepped forward, ready to finish the job the monsters from the deepest depths of our world had started all those years ago. I was alone. No one would know it was me who killed her. No one would ever know.

I licked my lips as I contemplated it. Yes. I'd waited for this day for five years. It would end a lot of pain and heartache for me.

*But what was she running from?*

I glanced at where she went, then back to her bedroom, grinding my teeth. Maybe I should just let the creature take her. Save me the blood on my hands. It was against our rules to kill a Nattie unless it was dire circumstances. Even if the Order found out I'd done it, I'd probably get off just because of how powerful I was. Straightening my spine, I made up my mind. I was going to do it. But I wanted to see for myself if she was being chased because something had brought me there. In the past, it was always some dark creature or a lost one— wandering dead—with her. It was never simple.

As I stepped into her dark bedroom, my red eyes narrowed. The air was thick with death. Something was there, lurking. I flung her closet door open. A switch turned on inside of me. Either for old time's sake, my desire to be the one to take her out, or my need for peace—whatever the reason, I was ready to fight it out with whatever creature there was. I frowned when I saw the closet was normal, containing nothing but clothes hanging.

"What the hell?" Puzzled, I backed out and looked around. I made my way to her bed and checked beneath it only to find the space empty of anything. There didn't appear to be anything there, but I could sense it. There was a broken picture frame on her desk, the shards of glass sparkling like diamonds in the moonlight.

"Come out, come out wherever you are," I growled, looking around. *There!* Out of the corner of my eye I saw it slide out from beneath her dresser. I lunged at it, my sword aimed to kill. It darted away, and I turned and watched as it faced me.

"You seek to protect what you should let die," it hissed at me. Its gnarled features were indiscernible in the darkness for the average Special. Thankfully, I was anything but. It had always been easy for me to see through the darkness. Tonight proved to be no exception. I knew exactly what *it* was—an ugly creature with razor-sharp teeth that could chomp through bone without having to bite twice. Its low purring growl and *click, click* of its claws on Everly's wooden floor showcased its impatience. It wanted to feed on her. To sink its teeth into her tender pink flesh and feast on all the deliciousness that came along with pretty, scared girls.

"Shows what you know," I growled at it, itching to plunge my sword through it so I could get to Everly in the next room. "It'll be *me* who kills her. Not you."

"You can't kill what you know you'll never let die, Shadow," it snarled at me. A hissing cackling erupted from it. "As for me, all you'll succeed in doing is sending me back to the Veil and buying her just a little more time because you won't kill her. You don't even realize how important she is. More of us will come for her. Thousands more."

"She's already dead as far as I'm concerned, wraith," I hissed in a deadly whisper. It chuckled darkly at me, it's mouth opening to reveal its rows of razor-sharp teeth.

"You know *nothing* of her, you stupid boy. Let me take her. Let me suck her sweet soul from her body. Save us both the time."

"Never. It's mine to take," I rumbled, done with the banter. I didn't wait to hear more from its forked tongue. I rushed forward, my anger and desire to be the one to take Everly driving my sword forward. It let out a nasty, gurgling shriek and darted through her bedroom wall before I could get to it.

I dashed out to the hall and caught sight of it sliding beneath the door I knew she was probably cowering behind. Firmly, I pushed the thought out of my mind. I knew she'd be scared, but I'd be swift in her death. I wouldn't make her suffer. *That* was a promise I could keep. I slipped through the door as silently as I could and surveyed the room. My eyes fell on her as she cowered in bed beside her sleeping mother, the blankets hauled up tightly around her, her plump pink lips moving in a silent plea.

I let out a gasp. When she'd rushed from her room. I hadn't gotten a good look at her. She was beautiful. In fact, she was the most beautiful girl I'd ever laid eyes on. My heart gave a painful jolt as I realized how badly I wanted to touch her ivory skin and soothe away her fears, rather than plunge my blade deep into her beating heart. She'd morphed into a gorgeous woman, growing into her long legs and arms. She stole my breath away. The wraith came up on its haunches and lunged at her, teeth bared, yanking me abruptly from my awe of the girl who sat trembling in her mother's bed. Racing forward, I pulled myself out from my silent reverie of her beauty and ran my sword through the creature as she let out a blood-curdling scream. Her pretty green eyes were wide with fright and locked on me.

I stared at her, warring with myself. Moments before, I wanted to end her. But now that I stood gazing at her, all I wanted was to rush to the terrified beauty and wrap her small trembling body in my arms, run my fingers through her silky, black locks, and hold her while I promised that everything would be OK. But I couldn't.

That wasn't how this was supposed to go! My hand twitched on my blade as I stared back at her. It would be quick. It would barely hurt. I'd never killed a Nattie before. I'd never had to. But this was different. My mother was dead because I'd rushed to save Everly. I took a step forward, swallowing hard.

*Do it! Kill her! End it!*

She stared at me, with tears streaming down her face as she sobbed. Her mother began to stir. I had to do it now. I raised my sword a fraction of an inch.

*Damnit!*

I let out a frustrated sigh, my hand loosening on the hilt of the blade. I couldn't. My heartstrings tugged as I stared at her. Instead, I backed away as her mother woke and held her. Everly's small, terrified voice babbled through her curtain of dark hair as her mother hugged her tightly, attempting to soothe her. It was all too reminiscent of a time long past.

I should've left. I knew I should have. Instead, I found my way back to her bedroom and sat down on the bed. The minutes swept past me, turning into hours. I was afraid to leave her and afraid to stay. I didn't know what I was capable of in either aspect. They wanted her—the dead, the undead, the dark creatures from the deepest, darkest pits of our world. I had no clue why, but I needed to find out if I was going to be able to make the decision that was tormenting me.

I picked up the broken picture frame and stared at her beautiful face. She was all smiles and bright eyes. My heart lurched. I tugged the photo out of its frame and stuffed it into my cloak pocket knowing that no matter what, I wanted to be able to see her face again.

# CHAPTER 3

$\mathcal{I}$ watched her from the shadows of her bedroom as she came in the next morning, her eyes bloodshot and her hair a wild mess. My vision last night hadn't done her justice. Everly Torres had grown into something extraordinary. I fought the urge to reach out to her, to either kiss those sweet lips of hers or shove my blade deeply into her chest. Even when I was twelve, I knew I wanted to kiss her. I only ever spoke to her that one time—the *last* time. Before that, fear kept me from conversing with her. I knew she could see me then, and I knew she was afraid of me, thinking that I was one of *them*. I had simply stood watch over her. Protecting her. Worrying for her.

But then I'd gone back and found my mother dead. So, I'd spent the last five years in a constant state of panic, confused about what I'd do if I ever saw Everly again. I had no idea why I'd been thrust into her world in the first place, but I knew there had to be a reason. Deep inside I wanted to believe one day she'd need me again. And when she did, I'd be there to finish what I prevented so long ago.

I let her leave the house, following behind her the best I could. Melding with the shadows was a gift I was especially good at. Being a member of the Conexus, we were one cohesive unit, each member sharing their strengths to the group, thus me giving my group the gift of shade—the ability to turn to shadow and shadow meld. All of my gifts were exceptional, making me an anomaly. We could also shimmer in and out of visibility so the Natties—the Naturals, people not Special like us—wouldn't see us. That worked well when we had to pursue the Cipher in public. To be fair, all Specials could remain hidden from the Nattie eye. It was one of the things we learned to do at Dementon.

The Order took me in at a young age and began training me, citing very early on that I'd one day become a Conexus general. By thirteen, I was a general, and my abilities began to manifest stronger with new ones cropping up every few months. Everyone who knew me figured I was a shifter, which was true. However, it meant more than what other people thought. I could shift like a normal shifter into creatures, but I could also shift my gifts to become a different Special—with the exception of vampire—a "gift" I'd never in a million years want anyway. I could be a lock—warlock—or a healer or anything else I wanted. No one knew of my gifts. No one, not even my best friends within Conexus knew what I was truly capable of.

My thoughts froze as Everly crossed the street and headed to the school grounds. Her head ducked low causing her dark hair to create a curtain over her pretty face. I slipped through the shadows of trees and followed her into the school, my curiosity over her eating at me like a hungry, insatiable monster. She must have been hungry because she grabbed a few items from the breakfast line before sitting down across from a pretty blonde girl.

"Hey, Nina." She let out a yawn. Her voice was as beautiful as she was. Feminine. Delicate. Soothing in my ears. I breathed out deeply, trying to get my head together. The girl was completely mesmerizing.

"You look exhausted." Nina's eyes swept over her worriedly. She cared deeply for Everly, that much was certain. "What's wrong? Is it Dylan?"

I bristled at the sound of his name. *Who the hell was Dylan, and what had he done to her?* I shook my sudden anger off, becoming irritated with myself for my feelings. *Ugh!* I pushed them away and shifted to be closer to her.

"No." Everly's plump lips turned down into a frown, her green eyes darkening.

"It's OK if it is. He was a total douchebag," Nina proclaimed. Everly's eyes traveled to a guy a few tables over as he laughed with his friends. An all-American looking guy with dark hair styled in a faux hawk and a tight polo shirt that showcased how much he worked out. I immediately hated him. He looked like the kind of guy who wouldn't appreciate Everly. The kind of guy who couldn't last even a round with me in the ring. Everything he had was just for show. The fact that I cared made me sick to my stomach.

"I don't care," Everly muttered, pushing the slice of toast and breakfast bar she was holding in her hands away. "He can have Brit. He *clearly* wanted her, so I guess we both win."

He'd really hurt her. The sorrow flowed from her, her sadness and heartbreak. It made me angry that he had. All I could think about was going to him in that moment and wrapping my fingers around his neck. Then squeezing until he apologized to her. I backed away from her, knowing if I stuck around, I'd have trouble controlling myself. Now, I was even more torn—my old feelings for her kicking the shit out of my hatred for her.

Besides, I'd been gone far too long as it was. I hadn't checked in with Conexus, and *that* was a hard and fast rule—my rule. And I'd broken it to spend the night at Everly's home. If she needed me again, I'd know. Then I'd come for her and do what I had to do. Plus, I'd just disappeared into thin air on the guys. I imagined my group had been frantic, going crazy with worry. Eric, being next in command, probably organized a search party and notified the Order of my disappearance in an attempt to find me.

I slinked deeper into the shadows and traveled quickly back to Dementon with my heart in my throat at having Everly back in my life because deep down, I *knew* she belonged to me. She always had. Even if I did hate her. She was mine.

# CHAPTER 4

"*D*ude, where the hell have you been?" Eric demanded, turning to me as I stepped in the commons of our dorm at Dementon. Everyone was gathered, all ten of them. A map of the area was laid out on the coffee table, and red tabs marked various places. They'd definitely been looking for me.

"We were leaving to go search for you. *Again*," Brandon folded his arms over his broad chest and stared pointedly at me as I removed my cloak. I didn't say anything as I walked deeper into the room. I wasn't even sure how to address everything. Whatever happened, still had me feeling shell-shocked. It didn't help that I couldn't seem to sort out my feelings properly.

"You freaking disappeared into thin air! Do you have any idea how worried we've been? We didn't hear from you all night! We were going to contact the Order!" Adam added, his dark eyes trained on me.

"Are you going to answer one of us?" Damien asked from his perch on the couch. "Seriously, Shadow, it's your rule that we always check in with one another. What happened to stop that last night? I mean, you were there, then you weren't. How the hell—you know what— just, *where* the hell were you?"

I went to my high-backed, black velvet chair and sat down in it, rubbing my face tiredly. I didn't know how to tell them what had happened. Eric and Damien didn't know about Everly. No one did, not even Amara, my werewolf girlfriend who was glaring at me with her lips pursed from a corner of the room beside Sloane, our caster. A sinking feeling filled my stomach. I'd forgotten about Amara.

"I can't explain it," I started, deciding I had to say something. Leaning forward, I rested my elbows on my knees and let my head hang down. I ran my fingers through my shaggy, silver hair in frustration. Internally, I tried to gather my thoughts before speaking. I had to choose my words wisely. "I was pulled to a Nattie home far from here. There I got caught up with a wraith. I followed it and managed to send it back to the Veil. In the process, I received intel that more will be coming—a *lot* more. We're going to need to start planning for them."

"A *wraith?*" Jared, a lock asked, his dark brows knit. "Why would a wraith appear at a Nattie home? That's one of the darkest creatures of our world. What's really going on, Shadow?"

"Should we be worried?" Chloe got to her feet, already tying her blonde hair up into a ponytail, ready to fight. That was the best thing about her, the werewolf was always ready to go. The girl had no fear, one of the reasons I chose her to join us—that and the fact that she could fight like crazy.

I drew in a deep breath and shook my head. *Why did they want Everly so bad?* I'd spent years trying to figure it out but had always come up empty-handed. Even her own father wanted to give her to them. And not just to wraiths. To the dead. *Why would the dead want her to join them? How was her dad able to see them and* not *be a registered Special?* It didn't make any sense!

"I don't know," I answered softly, a rush of foreboding coursing through me. "But I feel like it's going to be something big once I figure it out. I think we should start upping our training and start doing some research. I'm going to pay a visit to Xanan and speak to the Order. I'll check the registry to see if maybe the family is registered on our lists of Specials. Maybe I'll get some answers that way. I could even talk to Headmaster Brighton. For now, everyone just be extra careful. Classes are going to be ending here soon, so many of the students will be leaving. Those who don't, we need to make sure they're safe. Double up patrols. Make sure all entrances and exits are sealed. Sloane, I'm going to need you to make sure the wards are up. You, Adam, and Jared," I nodded to my resident warlocks and caster, "can make sure that gets done. Now."

They didn't question me. They scampered through the front door to complete the task.

"The rest of you, start putting together patrols. Let's get some investigating done. I want information on wraiths on my desk by sunrise. And get me the latest on Cipher nests. Go. Now."

Everyone left the room. Everyone except Eric, Damien, and Amara. A sigh huffed out my lips. I knew I wouldn't be able to get away from Amara. She'd been eyeing me from across the room, no doubt itching to bombard me with questions.

"Shadow," Amara's voice was small as she stared at me with her hazel eyes. A tilt of her head made her red hair tumble from her shoulders. Amara was completely gorgeous. Last spring, I'd started dating her after realizing how lonely I'd been. Guiltily, I stared at her as she stood close to me. The thoughts I'd had concerning Everly last night still running through my mind—the *good* thoughts about how beautiful she was, how I longed to hold her and kiss her, and tell her everything was going to be OK. I wasn't like that with Amara. In fact, recently I'd started to think that maybe I wasn't *normal* because I didn't have overwhelming feelings of love when I was with my girl-friend. I wasn't affectionate. I didn't long to kiss her or hold her. For the most part, I wasn't a touchy, huggy, and kissy kind of guy. I never had been. With *anyone*. Except with Everly. And even those feelings were marred by my hatred now. "I was worried about you."

"I'm fine," I stated evenly, my voice hard, a tactic I employed often to keep people at arm's length when I needed to be alone. And right now, I desperately needed to be alone. "Go tend to what I've told you to do."

"I missed you," she pressed with a sultry pout, her hands coming up to rest on my chest as she gazed up at me through her dark eyelashes. "I'm worried. The guys said you just disappeared. I want to know what's going on!"

"Amara," I said roughly. "We'll talk later. *Please.* You need to go."

She pouted for another moment before going up on her toes and planting a soft kiss on my lips. I half-heartedly kissed her back, my body not really excited for it at all. Honestly, I just wanted her gone. Before now, I'd at least feel a tiny smattering of hopeful butterflies whenever I kissed her. Or maybe it had simply just been me wanting to be *normal* with a girl for a change. Maybe I'd been lying to myself the entire time about my feelings. Now, with her lips pressed to mine, I had nothing, not even a tiny flutter. It caused me to worry. Something within me had changed in the last few hours. Any progress I'd potentially made over the last few months with Amara was flung from the highest tower and lay smashed at my feet.

"What's really going on?" Eric asked as Amara disappeared through the door. Both my friends stood staring at me, waiting for me to answer.

"I really *don't* know." I grew quiet. I had to tell them about Everly. I'd been friends with Eric and Damien since we were old enough to walk. We grew up together, fought together, and even been there for each other during the worst moments of our lives. I could trust them with anything.

"Do you remember when we were kids and I asked you guys if you thought it was possible for a Special to walk through the void and you guys laughed at me?"

"Yeah," Damien said, Eric nodding.

"I know the answer to it," I continued softly.

"*What?* What the hell's going on?" Damien demanded. I sighed and gestured for them to follow me into my office located off the commons. Eric closed the door behind him. Damien propped himself up on a couch near the fireplace and my desk.

"Come on, man," Eric encouraged, his blue eyes focused on me as I started pacing the room, something I always did when I was deep in thought.

"When I was four, I was in bed. The same thing happened to me then that happened to me last night. It wasn't nearly as bad... but I disappeared then, too."

Damien and Eric exchanged looks but didn't speak.

I launched into the story of Everly—telling them everything I knew about her, describing from the first time I saw her and ending with how the last time was in that closet after rescuing her when she was twelve. How I'd spent my childhood protecting her. How I'd come to care very deeply for her. And how I'd left my mother alone to save Everly that last time only to return to find my mother drained by a vamp.

"Is that where you were tonight?" Eric asked when I finished. "She drew you back to her?"

"Yeah." I nodded angrily as I saw my mother in my mind's eye, her pale body lying in the cold grass with her wildflowers scattered around her. "I spent the last five years thinking about her, hoping I'd get to see her again... so I could kill her."

"You want to *kill* her?" Eric asked, horrified, his blue eyes opening wide.

"It's against our laws to kill a Nattie," Damien cut in, just as shocked as Eric by my words.

"I know," I mumbled, running my fingers through my hair in frustration. "I didn't. I didn't even touch her. I left her."

"And? Was she OK?" Damien demanded, leaning forward to look at me. "I guess I should say, will she be OK, because you're talking like a madman."

"She's being terrorized by *something*. I disposed of the wraith. I don't know why it was there, but I do know that she's going to be needing me again. And I'll go and finish what should've been done ages ago."

"This is nuts," Eric whistled, shaking his head. "So, what are you going to do? Just walk in and kill her? What if the Order finds out? I'm sorry, man. I can't get on board with this. You can't go around killing innocent girls because you blame them for your mother's death. It's not her fault."

"It *is* her fault!" I snapped heatedly. "I'd have been there to save my mother if I hadn't gone to Everly! This is all her fault!"

"It's not," Eric returned evenly, not wavering in the slightest. He and Damien were the only ones in our group that could rival me, so I knew he wasn't afraid to go toe-to-toe with me. "She was just a kid. From what you've said, I highly doubt she even knew what was happening to her. It's not her fault. Not even a little. You need to push that shit aside and remember the girl you fell for because that's the same girl you're talking about *murdering*. And it would be murder. She's an innocent."

I let out a breath of frustration as I thought about Everly. Though I abhorred it, my heart ached for her. I knew if she died I wouldn't be able to survive without her. Even through the years I'd thought about her, and not just about killing her. Actually, I'd probably thought more about holding her than killing her. And I hated myself for it. It felt like I was betraying my mother because I let her die to save someone else.

"I'm going to take it to the Order. See if I can find out anything new about her. I didn't tell them when I was younger because I didn't think they'd believe me. But now, I'm in a better position to speak out. Maybe that'll help," I said finally.

"Being a general in the most elite group in Special history helps." Damien grinned at me.

"And you won't harm her?" Eric narrowed his eyes at me.

"I won't," I grunted, not really believing myself but knowing I didn't exactly have a choice. They were right. It was a huge crime to *harm* anyone, Natties included. *Did I really want that hanging over my head?*

"I wonder why she wasn't brought to Dementon back when all this started," Eric mused with a frown, accepting my answer without question. "She's clearly a Special."

"That's what I'm thinking too. But what *kind* of Special? What kind could pull someone from anywhere and bring them to their bedroom door?" I thought aloud.

"The kind I want to meet." Damien chuckled. I scowled, and Eric rolled his eyes at him.

"I'm not sure, but I'm going to get some answers." I was beyond frustrated.

"What about Amara?" Eric ventured. "You going to tell her about this girl who seems to have some sort of control over you?"

"I don't know." I shook my head. "You know how she gets. I know I need to tell her. Maybe I'll put it out there for her to know. Just don't say anything to anyone else about this. I'll explain it away for them once I have more answers."

"You know we got you, brother." Eric clapped me on the shoulder, making me feel a little more at ease.

"Don't you think it's odd that the Order hasn't brought her in?" Damien asked thoughtfully. He glanced at me for a moment before continuing, "I mean, if she doesn't already attend a Special school. Maybe there's a reason she hasn't been brought here. Maybe she's dangerous."

"She's not *dangerous*," I snorted at him, thinking about how small she was and remembering how scared she'd always been. "She's tiny and afraid."

"I'm not talking about size, man," Damien replied earnestly. "I'm talking about abilities. What is she capable of? Does she just *see* the dead or something? And if so, that's a bit of a big deal. Remember the Wards?"

"You can't possibly be suggesting what I *think* you're suggesting," Eric interrupted wide-eyed.

"He's right," I murmured. "A mancer can commune with the dead. Can walk in the Veil and *still* come back to life. Can bring the dead back to life." My breath caught in my throat as I thought about the possibilities of what she could be capable of if it proved to be true.

"What if she is one?" Damien pressed. "Then that means you're—"

"No." I shook my head firmly, my heart thrashing wildly in my chest. "No way. Not possible. This is speculation only. A mancer hasn't been born in centuries, and there's no history of a Reever *ever* being born. No one even knows if there is such a thing as reever. It's just from the Old Words."

"Shadow's right," Eric agreed tightly. "Let's just wait to see what

31

the Order has to say about it. There's no sense in getting upset over it right now."

A sick feeling roiled in my gut. Something about this whole situation seemed strange. I had to have the answers. These feelings I had for Everly were so overpowering that I was doing all I could to keep myself from going to her at that moment, and I knew I'd hold her more than I'd kill her, a feeling that tormented me inside.

"You look like you have something on your mind, Shadow," Damien commented.

I surveyed my friends silently for a moment. They were right. We'd known each other since we learned to walk. We trained together. Hunted together. Did everything together. Me withholding information on them wasn't like me.

"Something's changing," I said softly, swallowing hard. "I don't know what it is, but I can *feel* it. There's this... pull to her. She needs me. And-and I... think I need her. I can't describe it. I-I want to love her more than hate her."

"What do you mean?" Damien asked, unfolding his arms, a look of confusion on his face that mirrored Eric's.

"She's mine," I answered simply, knowing that was exactly what the feeling was. Everly was *mine*. She'd always been and always would be. Dead or alive, the girl belonged to me. Whatever that meant.

# CHAPTER 5

"*Yours?*" Eric asked, his confusion turning into concern.

"I feel for her," I murmured. "I always have. But now, it's different. I don't understand it. And it's killing me." Fear filled my eyes as I met each of their gazes. I'd never felt like that before. I'd never wanted to have that sort of relationship with anyone. Even with Amara it was forced and unnatural, but now...I wanted *her*. I wanted Everly. It was eating at me, warring with my hatred, confusing me, making me feel frantic and unpredictable.

"OK, hold up," Damien cut in, his hand in the air. "Are you telling us that you're in *love* with a girl you've never spoken to? I thought you hated her and wanted to kill her?"

"I'm not *in* love with her." I ran my fingers through my hair and rubbed my eyes, denying the strange swell of feelings bubbling up within me. "And I have spoken to her—once. And maybe my time with Amara is up. And I *do* hate her. I'm confused."

"Damn, brother. You're messed up. You're considering breaking it off with Amara, but you're telling us you're not in love with this other girl—what's her name again?" Damien looked at me skeptically.

"Everly. Her name is Everly."

"OK, so, Shadow. You're a bad ass. And you've been banging it out with one of the hottest chicks we've ever met—Amara. Then, out of the blue, someone you protected as a kid is back in the picture, a chick you've spoken to once..." He rolled his eyes. "...and who, in fact, is probably *terrified* of you since you have it in your mind that you want to kill her, and *now* you want to break it off with Amara to...*what*? If you don't love this chick, then what the hell is going on?" Damien leaned forward in his seat again and stared pointedly at me. "Tell me one thing, man."

"What?" I mumbled.

"How *hot* is this Everly chick?"

"Man, shut up." I shook my head at him. "It's not like that at all! This is something *different*. I told you. I'm drawn to her, and I think that part is winning over my desire to kill her."

"OK, chill, man. So, because of some weird *pull* you feel to the girl, you've decided to break things off with Amara? I'm sorry, brother. But that makes absolutely no sense to me," Damien finished. "You should probably get in touch with Brighton and see about getting your head examined. Too many hits from the carrion may have left you punch drunk." He imitated being punched in the head.

"I think what Damien is *trying* to say..." Eric shot a sour look at Damien. "...is that you may be reacting rashly here. Breaking it off with Amara probably *isn't* the best choice right now. Maybe you just need to figure out what the deal is with this girl. Go to the Order. See what they say. They may have all the answers you need. Once you know what's going on, then make the decision. For now, just go let your girl show you how much she missed you. She's been driving us nuts. And I'm going to be honest, you're acting all sorts of crazy. Maybe you just need to get laid and relax for a bit. Couldn't hurt at this point."

"You're right," I said, climbing to my feet. "I'm reacting poorly. I-I just don't know what's happening to me. I'm *not* this guy."

"It's cool, man. I'd be confused too if this stuff was happening to me." Eric gave me a grin. "But to set the record straight, Amara may be hot, but I can't stand her. I'm not the one who has kiss her ass though. That, and all these choices, are on you, friend."

"Thanks, ass." I shook my head, giving him a playful shove. We ended the meeting, and I made my way outside and found Amara in the school square with a sour look on her pretty face. I wanted to feel something with her. *For* her. I wanted to experience with her what I sensed with Everly—not the hatred part. The part where it felt like my soul was singing for her. I'd never had a *real* conversation with Everly, but I knew if I ever did, she would astound me. With Amara, it was always so... dry. She was high maintenance, and sometimes I wondered if she only wanted me because of who I was.

"Hey," I called out as I stopped beside her. Her lips curved up into a smile at my presence. But still there was *nothing*, not even a dash of butterflies in my gut.

"Hey. Did you guys get everything worked out?"

"Yeah," I said, squinting my eyes, the sun far too bright for my liking.

"I didn't get much information," Amara continued, clearing her throat. "I couldn't focus."

"That's not acceptable," I answered sternly. "When you're asked to complete a task, you must, even if your mind is elsewhere. It's part of being what we are, Amara."

"Like you?" she countered. "You disappeared and ran out on the guys! What's that all about?"

"What I do on my own missions is *no* concern of yours," I growled, my already growing frustration rearing its ugly head as I stared down at her. "And it wasn't like I had a choice in the matter."

"I want to know what's going on," she demanded, her lower lip jutted out. "You're always so secretive! I'm your *girlfriend*! I deserve to know—"

"Amara," I said firmly, looking around to see a few students were staring at us interestedly. The moment they noticed me noticing them, they hastily tried looking busy. That was how things were for me—people feared me, as they should. I wasn't exactly the most engaging guy, and I enjoyed being what I was. I steered Amara out of the square and down a small alley before speaking again. "Something is happening. Something *big*. I don't know why or what it is. I just know things are going to change soon. You're a member of Conexus. You *know* when missions come, we do them without question. Even the ones we don't want to do." I considered what was happening with Everly to be a mission, even if it wasn't handed down by the Order. I had the power of Conexus on missions as long as they were justified. *This* was justified.

"What are you saying?" She frowned at me.

"I'm saying that just be prepared and don't hate me."

"You're scaring me, Shadow," she murmured, her hands coming out to rest on my chest as she stared up at me. "I love you."

I shook my head and looked away, not saying anything. Those words meant something to her, but not to me. I hated it when we had those conversations. *Why couldn't we just have some fun and relieve some stress without it always turning so serious?* Every touch, every kiss, every time we were near each other had to be some big gesture where words that didn't mean shit to me being forced on me. It seemed like every time we were together anymore it turned into *this.*

"Why don't you ever say it back to me?" she asked softly, her bottom lip trembling. "I've said it countless times, and you've never said it back to me once."

"Amara..." I took her shaking hands in mine, hating the person I was. "I'm sorry. I'm just not in the same place you are."

"You will be though, right?" Her eyes flashed fearfully. "Because we only have each other—" She was so dramatic.

"I don't want to have this conversation right now," I mumbled, reaching out and brushing her red hair away from her face. It was the most effort I could put into the moment and even *that* was difficult. "You know how I feel about this stuff."

"I know, but I need to know that *this* is going somewhere! All you do is cater to the Order—"

"The Order is my life," I growled, pushing her hands away from me. "It's my *entire* future. I'm a general, Amara. I'm next in line as the sigil! I was born into this. I'm royal. The Order comes first. *Always.* You should know that better than anyone."

"You'd choose it over love?" she whispered, her hazel eyes filling with tears. I closed my eyes for a moment, Everly's beautiful face dancing in the darkness. *Why was I seeing her face? Why was she haunting me? Why was my heart beating madly in my chest at just the thought of her?* God, she was seriously messing my head up.

"I don't know. Right now, it's my main focus. We're fighting a war. The safety of everyone—Specials, Natties, our worlds—is the most important. The Cipher are out to get us and take over. You know how important it is now more than ever for us to remain focused on our tasks."

"I get that. I do!" She wrapped her arms around me and rested her head against my shoulder. She was a tall girl, as were most female werewolves her age. I pictured holding Everly in my arms, how her head would probably rest perfectly on my chest. In my mind, Everly was my puzzle piece, fitting perfectly against me like she was made for me and me for her.

*Damnit. What the hell!*

I gave myself a quick mental shake. I had to figure out why I was feeling so much for her when I'd only spoken to her once. When I blamed her for my mother's death. It wasn't in my nature to form such a close bond with *anyone*. To even try a relationship with Amara was practically unheard of with me.

I didn't hug her back. I never did, at least not in a way that would melt her heart. Maybe a quick pat here or there, but I never held her until she melted in my arms. Even kissing wasn't something I engaged in a lot. As for the rest, I wasn't the cuddle afterwards sort of guy either. I was the *"thanks-for-the-good-time-where-are-my-pants-I-have-to-go-now"* kind of guy. I still couldn't figure out why Amara wanted to be with me. I wasn't a wealth of emotion or affection. Damien liked to say she was attracted to my status, my crown, not *me*, because let's face it, I wasn't a good boyfriend.

"Will you *please* tell me where you went?" she begged softly as she gazed up at me.

I stared at her for a moment before letting out a sigh. I'd said I wasn't going to do this, yet here I was, in the midst of starting an argument over something neither of us could control. It wasn't like I *asked* to be drawn to Everly. I mean, not at first, but now that I was... I wanted to keep going. At least until I finished what I had to do, whatever that may be.

"There's this girl," I started. She immediately tensed. Amara wasn't cool with me talking to other girls. She had a jealous, mean streak which was typical of her kind, the werewolves. However, hers was just a little more pronounced with me. "We've been a part of each other's lives since we were little." I went on to explain the story of me and Ever to her. Her lips turned down into a deeper frown the further into the story I went. And she was all but scowling when I finished telling her the story of Everly.

"You've only ever spoken to her once?" she asked, her voice tight.

"Yes," I answered simply. "I wouldn't even know what to say to her if I did speak to her. I have to go to the Order to find out why she wasn't brought here as a child instead of being forced to exist with her gifts in the Nattie world. There's obviously a reason she and I are linked to one another—"

"You aren't *linked* to her!" Amara proclaimed, a dark cloud storming over her pretty features. "You're mine. You're linked to *me*. It's me and you, remember? You can't just go demand to know why the Order left her in the Nattie world. There's clearly a reason! Maybe she's crazy! And you just said it yourself, she's the reason your mother is dead."

I flinched at her words.

I quickly reeled in my anger. "Amara, you're acting insane. You need to chill," I reprimanded her softly, swallowing hard. "This is a matter that needs looking into, which is what I intended on doing. Everly...she's a quiet girl with no known mental issues, and she needs help. Maybe mine. I'm not sure. And I desperately need to figure out what's happening in my head. So, I'm going to do whatever I have to do whether I have your approval or not."

"So, you're going to do this no matter what I say?" Her lips were drawn tightly together as she surveyed me with cool eyes. "Even if I tell you that I don't want you to? Even if you decide she needs saving, and you're the one to do it?"

"Yes," I answered. "Even then. It's my duty to keep the peace, to keep people safe. My thoughts as of late haven't showcased it, and for that I'm ashamed. She's special to me." Her face fell with my words. They probably came out sounding more severe than I intended or portrayed more feelings toward Everly than I planned, even if those feelings were confusing to me.

"She's special to you, and I've been with you for nearly a *year* now and you've not once said anything close to that about me. We sleep together. We spend time together," her voice hitched. "But you *never* say things like that to me. I just want you to really sit back and think about me and you. Please?"

"Amara, I'm considering *killing* this girl. Do you understand that? I want to slice into her tender skin and watch her bleed simply because I blame her for my mother's death when I *know* I shouldn't. And on the flipside of it, I want to keep her safe from everything—including myself. I'm not standing here telling you that I'm in *love* with her." I breathed out, my heart aching beyond words for reasons I didn't want to explore. It was an unfamiliar feeling to me, and I didn't like it. "I'm telling you this is a serious situation where I may react in ways that could cost me everything. A-And I'm afraid for her. And me."

"Where am *I* in this picture? You're not even stopping to see how this affects *me*! We're together, Shadow. Me and you. Anything that happens to you, happens to me—"

"Mara, you know damn well we're just two people sleeping together. We haven't been linked in the ceremony like some of our other members. It's just me. And it's you. *Not* us. And we're totally separate when it comes to this. Get it through your head!"

"No! You always do this! You're always rushing to the aid of someone else! You were there for Sloane when she was inducted into Conexus. And then that Fae on campus a few weeks ago that was trying to learn to hold her damn sword? It was you at her side, trying to help! But when *I* need you, you're not there for me!"

"Why do you do this? If I'm not kissing your ass all the time, you're mad. What do you want from me, Mara? Huh? Because I'm not the guy you have in your head. Stop putting me up on some imaginary pedestal and hoping that I'll change! I'm *not* going to change. This is me. You knew that when you crawled into my bed. I can't even hang out with the guys and unwind. I'm at a breaking point here, and all you're concerned about is how it affects you. Cut the crap. I don't have the time or patience for it. I have way too much going on right now to deal with this shit."

"You know what? I don't have time to deal with it either!" she snapped at me, backing away. "In fact, go do whatever it is the great and mighty Conexus general has to do! I don't want to even talk to you until you get your shit together!"

She stormed off, her red hair whipping angrily behind her, leaving me standing alone in the alley. And for some reason, that didn't bother me.

# CHAPTER 6

*I* woke up early the next morning and dressed quickly. I'd sent a fire message to the Order the previous night asking about Everly and whether she was a registered Special. So far, I hadn't heard back from them. Before I fell asleep last night, I vowed to pay them a visit if I hadn't received word from them by morning.

I went to the basement of our home and pressed my hand to the ornate black portal gate on the wall. The runes lit up, and the opening glowed briefly before the lush greenery from Xanan became visible through it. Being able to portal to Xanan, a place located between Ireland and the United Kingdom in a place no Nattie could see, was a relief since getting there by other means took a long time. Usually, a strong caster or lock was needed to open the portal but since I seemed to possess that ability from them, I was able to open it without a hitch.

Eric, Damien, and I had grown up in the capital city of Xanan. We'd run through the rolling green fields on the edge of the realm, laughing and playing and poking all the magical creatures we could find. The memories of our days there brought a smile to my face.

"We've been expecting you," Danan, a member of the Sentries, a group of guards who kept watch over the Citadel—the meeting place of the Order—greeted me as I exited the portal outside Xanan's walls.

"Have you?" I asked, raising an eyebrow at him.

"Indeed." He nodded. "The Order said you'd be coming. Are you well, General?"

"Quite," I answered, not in the mood to talk to the overly interested man. It was no secret that Danan had desperately wanted to be a member of Conexus but never wowed any of the leaders in such a way to lead him to our ranks. Instead, he now headed the Sentries, the guards for the Citadel. It was like rent-a-cop for the Special world.

"It must be a very important visit to find you here so early in the day," he continued, glancing at me from the corner of his eye. I took the reins to one of the horses from him and hoisted myself up as he climbed on his horse. I remained quiet as he tried to dig information out of me. "Sir Sangrey has been looking forward to seeing you again. You're all he talks about."

Sir Sangrey was like a father to me. Though, he was my father's half-brother, he treated me more like a son than my own father had. He'd taken me under his wing early in my childhood when my abilities had started to rival his. As a powerful shifter, he was feared by many. His skills on the battlefield had wowed me at a young age, and I wanted to be just like him when I grew up. He was one of the people who truly pushed me to my full potential, and I owed him a lot.

When I didn't answer him, Danan continued, "I heard you and the she-wolf have grown rather close. Her father has applied for a spot on the council."

That was news. Amara hadn't mentioned her father being interested in joining the Order. But it didn't exactly surprise me, nor would him gaining the twelfth spot on it since it was open due to Sir Daris retiring to the Highlands—a plains region in the Fae realm where he hailed from.

"I hope Mr. LaCroix gets it," I stated as the horses carried us to the capital.

"Perhaps you should put in a good word for him," Danan suggested as we entered the gates to the sprawling city. I jumped from the white horse while Danan climbed off his tan one. As we entered the city, I looked around. The place was massive with stone buildings and cobblestone streets. It had grown darker in the last few years because the sunshine didn't reach all the places it once did. Eric told me I was imagining things, but I knew I wasn't. I blamed it on the war with the Cipher. It was sucking the energy out of all of us.

"Is that what you're here for?" Danan's voice broke into my thoughts.

"Excuse me?" I asked, having tuned him out.

"I asked if you were here to speak for LaCroix. I assumed since you and his daughter have been seeing one another, that was your reason. I heard that you two were… um… quite smitten. There's even talk of a wedding."

"*What?*" I frowned. "There's no wedding on the horizon, and I'm here on Conexus business."

"No wedding?" Danan grinned at me, infuriating me. "I hear things, you know. If LaCroix makes council, the sigil will *want* you to marry the she-wolf. You're both Conexus. Both your fathers are powerful men. It would unite the weres with the shifters permanently—"

We'd reached the entrance to the Citadel, a sprawling building with towers and turrets. The Order met on the other side of the doors. And just beyond the massive building sat the castle, my home as a child. My heart clenched tightly in my chest. I didn't come home often. With my mother no longer there, there really wasn't a point in it.

"You're not *denying* the wedding—"

"There is *no* wedding," I snapped, glowering at the man as his incessant talking took me to the edge of my sanity. "I am *not* engaged to Amara. I have no intentions of marriage anytime soon, and even if I did, *I* choose my bride, not the council."

"My apologies," he replied, not looking the least bit apologetic as he sneered at me. I ground my teeth in an effort to avoid punching him in the throat.

"Your weapons, General," two armed guards greeted me. I quickly unloaded all my knives, swords, and weapons, smirking at the fact they thought they were disarming me.

"You do realize I could take all three of you out with just a flick of my wrist, right? No weapon needed," I snarled, already irritated for having to listen to Danan the duration of the trip into the city. The men flinched, knowing damn well I spoke the truth.

"Ah, our finest Conexus general!" a voice boomed out. I turned and grinned to see Sir Sangrey coming through the doorway with his lips tipped up and his dark robes billowing behind him.

"Uncle," I greeted him with a handshake and a quick one-armed hug.

He pulled away from me and held me at arm's length. "You get bigger every time I see you, my boy! I heard you dispatched an entire nest of carrion. Impressive!"

"I didn't do it alone. I had my men with me."

"Always the modest one." Sangrey smiled. "I heard you out here threatening the guards. I figured I'd best come out and ensure you didn't hold fast to your word."

"I just don't understand what disarming me will do. You know as well as I do—"

"It's protocol, General. You know that," Sangrey continued, his dark eyes shining with mirth. "Come. I know you have much to discuss if you traveled all the way here so quickly."

I walked through the doorway with him.

"Your father is eager to see you."

"I very much doubt that," I answered dryly. My father and I had a rocky relationship. I never wanted what he wanted. If not for Sangrey, I probably would've rebelled against him and just been content staying in the background. My father wanted to parade me around like a prized show dog while I wanted to remain in the shadows. Having people know I was his son made me feel like I'd be judged by *that* rather than my own abilities, so we agreed to keep it under wraps with only the Order knowing who I was. Them, and my Conexus members.

"Did you hear LaCroix is up for councilman?" Sangrey asked as we walked down the stone hallway.

"I did," I answered tightly.

"He could use your vote. I assume you'll give it. It'd be a good idea considering you *are* dating his daughter."

"Dating, *not* marrying." I wanted to clarify that. Marriage was the furthest thing from my mind.

"For now," Sangrey commented mildly.

"What are you talking about?" I came to a halt.

"Your father is in talks with Benton LaCroix about your marriage to his daughter. I thought you knew that..." His studied me with his dark eyes, the fine lines around them crinkled, concern written on his face.

"I was not aware," I growled. "And I am not interested."

"Forgive me, I thought you loved the girl."

"I do not. She keeps my bed warm, Sangrey. I haven't felt nor spoken the words to her that all women desire to hear. Nor will I."

"I see." Sangrey nodded. "This is a problem, I'm afraid."

"Not for long," I started walking again, now with two pieces of business to address.

# CHAPTER 7

$\mathcal{I}$ was not in a good mood by the time I reached the Circle, the place where the Order met within the Citadel. The curved front of the circular room was where the various factions of the Order sat. There was space for other members of our world to gather whenever there were trials.

"General, it's a pleasure to see you. We were expecting you," Sir Broderick proclaimed as I stood in the center of the room facing them. They looked so official with their dark robes in place.

"I'd hope so," I growled. "I sent two fire messages. I didn't receive a response, so I figured I'd just pop in and see if the Cipher had finally torn this place down stone by stone."

"As always, full of charm and wit," Sir Broderick replied, his lips tight beneath his graying beard. The man came from a long line of pure blood locks, something he liked to remind people of whenever he got the opportunity.

"General, we received your fire messages," Sir Malek, an elderly Fae with long silver hair said from his seat among the panel, his dark eyes curious.

"I heard," I answered dryly.

"We assumed you'd make it a point to simply pay us a visit since that's usually your way," Sir Parsons, another lock, chimed in from where he sat. "But we planned on replying if we didn't hear from you by today."

"Good thing I'm so punctual," I said evenly, my gaze leveled on him. He gave me a small smirk.

"You have questions," the man in the center stated. He had hair black as pitch, just like Sangrey. However, smatterings of gray were sprinkled throughout. I looked at him and nodded. My father. We didn't have a close relationship. He liked to give orders, and I hated taking them, but it seemed to become one of my better habits as of late—taking orders without question. Our relationship had only gotten worse since the death of my mother. She was the one who held us together. Without her, we were just two angry men who blamed one another for her demise.

"The girl—Everly Lucia Torres—I suspect without question is a Special. I want to know if she's registered on our list of Specials. And if so, I want to know why she hasn't been brought to Dementon to have her skills honed. The girl suffers and has for years."

"The girl is not registered. But more importantly, General, how do you know she's suffered for years?" My father cocked his head at me. I swallowed hard and let my eyes wander over the councilmen who were all looking at me peculiarly. She wasn't registered. Something was wrong with that picture.

*How had she slipped through?* She had to have old blood. Specials just didn't *happen* without magical blood somewhere in their family.

"Because..." I breathed out deeply, hating myself for what I was about to tell them. Suddenly, it felt wrong. She needed me, and I felt like I was about to betray her. I knew if I could just get her to Dementon for help then maybe she'd be safe. Maybe she'd find herself and turn out to be worth the sacrifice. I'd be able to protect her more easily. Watch over her. We would keep an eye on her—all of Conexus. She could be trained. In that moment, I decided she needed to come prove herself at Dementon, and if this was the way to do it, then so be it. I had to tell them what she was, that she could see and speak to the dead. "Everly is a whisperer. I've been drawn to her since I was four years old."

I was greeted with silence. A palpable silence.

"Are you certain?" Sir Broderick asked breaking the silence.

"I'm pretty sure," I snapped. "I was tugged from my bed at four and visited her daily until she was twelve."

"Really? And why did the visits stop?" Sir Malek, a were, asked while the rest of the councilman stared at me.

"I don't know," I answered helplessly. "She blocked me. I was unable to find her. She moved. Her abusive father was taken away. Maybe she didn't need me beyond that time." I didn't tell them I blamed her for my mother's death, so maybe it was me who ended the visits. I didn't know why they ended, but it was probably a good thing they had.

"And now? You must have found her again, General," my father said easily.

"I *felt* her," I murmured. "It was a strange feeling. It washed over me. Drew me to her. Pulled me in. I had no choice in the matter. She's moved. She lives with her mother now. Wraiths were around. One was in her bedroom. It attacked her. I sent it back to the void."

"A *wraith*?" Sir Malek asked, surprised. "Are you certain?"

"Do you really need to ask me that question?" I demanded angrily. "I *know* my void walkers. It was a wraith."

"Wraiths are rare... They follow commands... Interesting," my father murmured with the councilmen.

The thought hadn't slipped my mind. Wraiths didn't just wander around for fun. They always had a purpose.

"What are you asking of us?" Sangrey asked, his deep voice booming out and silencing the room. He stared impassively at me. He didn't like for the Order to know of his loyalty to me.

"I think you need to bring her to Dementon."

"No," Sangrey stated without explanation.

Staring hard at him, I asked, "Why not?"

"Well, General," Sangrey continued, steepling his fingers as he surveyed me. "Do you not know the Old Words? I'd think someone of your position would be well-acquainted with them."

"You mean the texts pertaining to the Wards?" I asked, frowning as a sickness washed over me. Eric, Damien, and I already discussed this. I didn't want it to be true. God, I didn't.

"Yes. Those very ones. You said yourself that Everly's a whisperer."

"Those prophecies were recorded by the Fae long ago. Who knows if the Wards are even accurate? I mean a mancer hasn't been born in hundreds of years, and the last suspected one never had a reever, so when she died she stayed dead. A reever has never existed. *Ever*." I referred to the Old Words, stories of how a mancer—a Special who could commune with the Veil—coupled with a reever could raise an undead army. The two would create a never-ending cycle of life between the two of them. But Everly couldn't be a mancer. The thought of her being forced to live her life running from ghosts made me ill. A fresh wave of protectiveness like the one I used to have for her rushed over me.

"Think," my father growled at me, sitting forward in his seat. "You've been pulled to the girl. You know yourself to be different. Stronger. *More*. Don't you think it's *odd* that we have a Special with such strong abilities surface all of a sudden like this? We should probably keep a close eye on the situation considering what it could mean if the two of you *are* part of this prophecy. If you two are even remotely close to being what the prophecy spoke of, we *all* need to be keeping a closer eye on things. A mancer in the hands of our enemy would be very bad indeed. And you, what if you *had* to go simply because she was taken? We don't know how this works. We have to be cautious. We only know what some old fool bellowed out during a trance. We know that *she* fits what we know. She was born two hundred or so years after the death the fourth suspected mancer. Her birthday is in May. She's a whisperer. And we know she *could* be very dangerous. These things all meet the Rule of Five from the prophecy. As for you, you'd have to follow her to death *unless* you decided she wasn't worth saving."

I swallowed hard and drew in a deep breath.

"I am no *reever*," I snarled in denial. "If that's what you're thinking, you're wrong. I'm a general. Someday a councilman to the Citadel. A sigil. I'm no answer to prophecy. I refuse."

"Well, I don't believe you get a choice in it if it turns out to be true," Sangrey chuckled softly, sending a shiver of foreboding through my body.

"So, is that why she's been kept from Dementon?" I demanded. "Because of what she *might* be?"

"No." Sir Broderick sighed, rubbing his tired eyes. "She has been on our radar, as are all potential Specials who show signs. And her abilities *did* disappear at twelve. With whisperers, it's different than with other Specials. Some Nattie children can see into the Veil. Usually that gift disappears as they grow older. We assumed that Miss Torres was simply a Nattie whose abilities left her as she aged. The fact that she's tugged you back *and* the creatures are back for her, even the nasty ones like the wraiths, means what I fear—that she's stronger and an actual Special who is untrained. She *does* need to be brought to Dementon. It'll just be very late in her education which means she'll have to have extra training. That is, if we agree to allow her to attend. I feel like we need more information on the girl before we can make that decision. Perhaps she truly is nothing. And we don't want to waste our time or resources on a nothing Nattie." It was no secret that some of the councilman thought very poorly of the Nattie world, Sir Broderick being one of them.

"I agree," Sir Moran, a shifter who'd been silent, finally spoke up with a nod of his head, his beady eyes focused on me. "We cannot have an untamed Special, especially if she's what we think she might be, running amuck out there. If the Cipher get wind of this, it could spell disaster. Even if she isn't *the* Mancer, the girl may require help honing her abilities. She could be a very good asset to Conexus. You only possess one of the psychic faction within your ranks, correct?"

"That is correct," I said through clenched teeth. Eric was from the psychic faction. He wasn't all that great at predicting or seeing, but he had skills where they mattered with his telekinesis and stitching—the ability to stop time for a moment. I didn't want Everly in my ranks.

The thought of her out there fighting, killing, made me sick. I didn't want my life for her. She deserved freedom and happiness. I didn't want her near me past her being within Dementon's walls. "I don't believe there's another psychic out there worthy of Conexus ranking."

"You and me both. Eric Craft is a rarity all his own. He's unrivaled. " Sir Broderick nodded. "It's rare to find one that's gifted enough to be considered more than an entertaining way to pass the time. However, if this girl develops these gifts—true psychic gifts—she'd be an asset to more than just Conexus. She could turn the tide of the war for us. Her predictions could enable us to be a step *ahead* of the Cipher."

There was a general murmur of agreement within the group of men. My jaw clenched as I ground my teeth. It was bad enough inducting and training new members every year. It would be even worse with someone like Ever. She had *zero* knowledge of anything. It would be a nightmare.

"Have you spoken to the girl?" Sir Mathis, another shifter, asked, dragging me from my thoughts on how to keep her out of Conexus.

"Only once. When we were twelve. The last time I saw her. I told her I'd protect her. It was the only time we've ever spoken."

"I see." Sir Mathis sat back in his seat, steepling his fingers. Silence filled the room. My pulse roared in my ears. I was about to lose my cool with these guys.

"And what's more, our dear general here may be her reever," Sir Sangrey said, calmly breaking the silence. I looked at him and frowned. An unfamiliar glint flickered in his eyes. He seemed almost... *happy* about the situation. "There's really only one way to find out if you two are what we think you may be."

"You want to *kill* her?" I demanded, my hands beginning to twitch. "Just to test her? To test me? And if you're wrong?" Sangrey was never so bold. He was pissing me off, a rarity between the two of us. I should've been angrier at myself because only hours before I'd had my hand on my *own* blade ready to end her life. I was disgusting. My actions made me sick as I listened to the men before me devise a plot to reveal what she was. Hearing it from the other end made me realize how insane I'd been.

"Then she dies. She's a just Nattie who didn't make it. If you bring her back, then she'll become Order property." Sir Broderick nodded thoughtfully, completely unaware of the terror churning in my soul. Abuzz moved around the Order. "Besides, I can't imagine living her life is much fun. Killing her might do the poor thing a favor. And if she comes back, it'll be a bonus."

"No," I snarled, balling my hands into fists. My heart broke at the thought of anyone killing her. "I won't let that happen. Even if she *is* a Nattie, we're sworn to protect them as well as our own. Testing her by killing her is unacceptable." I had a new resolve for her life.

"How defensive you are of a girl you've only spoken to once," Sir Mathis mused. "That only further proves our point."

"Give me time. Let me investigate this further. I'll send my best men out to keep an eye on her to ensure she doesn't fall into the hands of the Cipher."

"And if she is what we think? You do realize she'll join Conexus, correct?" Sir Malek asked.

"I understand she would be *considered* but ultimately I have the control over who joins my ranks. And I only take the best," I snarled at the old men before me. It was an honor to be a part of Conexus, but Everly was meant to be free. I could feel it in my body when I looked at her. In my heart. She was meant for more than becoming a soldier.

"If she's a mancer, she'll be the best. She will be your other half if you are the reever. You already care for the girl. I can hear it in your voice when you speak," Sir Sangrey said the last word with a crisp snap of the syllables. "And you haven't been paired yet. Wouldn't you like to have the power that could come with pairing with your other half if it proves to be true? Ah, what an army we'd have."

I ground my teeth together, not saying a word. It took me a moment to collect myself.

"We cannot simply bring the girl to Dementon. She seemingly has no familial history of Special ability. Informing her family of her potential magical ability puts us under the Nattie radar. Perhaps a little coaxing from Headmaster Brighton may help the situation along. He runs the facility. If we're lucky, the girl will snap out of terror and end up there. From there, we can intervene and bring her here," my father stated. But he didn't sound all that sold on the idea. "In the meantime, *I* will personally look further into the girl's lineage and see if she has ancestors who've been registered or overlooked."

I nodded, accepting that my father had decided to personally take it upon himself to look into the matter. "Do you grant me permission to watch over the girl with my members or do I do it anyway?" I demanded evenly, my voice deep and threatening. The idea of Everly going crazy made me sick. "Because I'm only asking out of respect for you. I'll be doing it regardless."

My father answered without waiting to hear the council's thoughts, "Watch the girl. Report back any changes to us. If something happens to her—let's just hope you can bring her back or you're going to lose quite a talented Special."

"Nothing will happen to her," I vowed, that new resolve taking over as I saw her face flash in my mind. "I'll die before it does."

"That's what we're hoping for," Sir Broderick's dark voice rang out sending a chill down my spine.

# CHAPTER 8

*a*s I left the Circle, my body shook with anger. *They were gunning for her to die just to prove a point!* I'd never been so infuriated in my life, and a lot had to do with my own terrible, murderous thoughts. The moment Sangrey came out the door, I got in his face.

"What the hell was that?" I demanded angrily.

"Calm yourself, General. You know as well as I do there's something *off* about the entire situation with the girl," Sangrey answered smoothly. "I know you're upset. Try to see it from our point of view. If she is indeed the mancer, it could spell disaster for us if she falls into the wrong hands. I'm all for you watching out for the girl. And I know you are too. I can tell how deeply you care for her whether or not you choose to admit it."

"Which you best get out of your head right now," my father's deep voice cut in as he came through the doors, his dark robes billowing behind him and his eyes narrowed at me. "I've entered into talks with Benton LaCroix on your behalf to marry his daughter, Amara. It would be a smart match for the both of you. I don't see the issue with it since you've been with the girl for nearly a year. I'm sure you've gotten to know her both inside and out." His eyes glinted with dark humor, making me angry.

"*No one* decides who I will marry," I snapped.

"Wrong. I will," my father returned. "I'm the sigil. I'm your father, and you're a soldier. A general. The future sigil. You *will* do what you're told, or I'll bring you to the dungeons and beat some sense into you."

"You could try," I hissed, taking a dangerous step toward him, ready to throw down right then if need be. Sangrey got between us.

"General," he warned as my father glared at me over Sangrey's shoulder. "Walk away. Perhaps a visit to see your mother is in order. It's been a long time since you've been to visit her site."

"She's dead," I bit out sourly. "My presence at a box won't change that."

"She's dead because *you* failed to keep her safe," my father snarled at me, pushing Sangrey aside. "She's dead because the life was sucked from her by the Cipher vampire! All because you failed to protect her! Because you left her!"

"Me?" I laughed bitterly. "You keep pointing the blame at me, *but where were you?*"

A muscle thrummed along his jaw. He wanted to hit me, but he knew if he did, I wouldn't hold back, and *that* would be a blood bath for the both of us.

"Do you think she'd want this?" I hissed, glaring at him. "Do you think she'd want me to marry someone I don't love just like she was forced to do? Because let's face it, *that* never made anyone happy."

He flinched like I'd struck him. I couldn't stop. "She'd hate the idea. You *know* she would." I snorted bitterly at him.

He frowned deeply. I couldn't say my parents were unhappy. My mother always supported my father, even seemed like she loved him. But I knew it hurt her to not marry who she wanted. She was a romantic. And there was nothing romantic about marrying someone you didn't love. And then she was killed by a Cipher vampire while out picking flowers on the edge of the kingdom. A simple task she loved doing every Sunday evening. And that simplicity had gotten her killed when a rogue stumbled upon her. I found her body later that evening after I returned from Everly. She'd been completely drained of blood, her wildflowers scattered around her lifeless body.

"She knew what it took to rule a world!" my father snapped back at me. "If you had half the sense she did, we wouldn't be having this conversation right now!"

"To hell with this," I spat, backing away. "I won't marry Amara. I won't. No one decides my fate. No one."

I turned and swept from the Citadel, fuming.

And through all my angry thoughts, the only thing I could see was Everly's beautiful face. Jumping on the horse I'd ridden into the city, I urged him to gallop to the palace gates. I was allowed in without issue. I leaped off and made my way behind the castle to the crypts just beyond it.

The guards gave me a nod and moved aside as I passed through. I knew where she lay—a golden ornate coffin in the center of the room. Alone I looked down at her resting place. Lifting my hand, I gave it a small flick. A red and gold swirl of magic came forth. I twisted my hand and didn't stop until I held her favorite flower in my hand—a daisy. She loved wildflowers, which was what caused her to go pick them. I placed it on her coffin, my eyes burning with unshed tears. I let my hand rest on the cold box, my anger and sadness ebbing through me. I didn't cry. The last time I had was when she was put into the royal crypt. I'd grown colder, harder, angrier that day. It was the day I vowed to end Everly.

I remembered the last time I saw my mother like it was yesterday.

*"You should wear your cloak, Fin," she admonished me, using her nickname for me, a grin on her lips as her green eyes sparkled. "You're going to be so cold!"*

*"Mother." I shook my head, serious. "I don't get cold."*

*"Oh, my sweet son," she chuckled, ruffling my silver hair with her fingers. "Please? Humor your mother. You know how much I worry for you." Her smile had disappeared only to be replaced with a fearful look, her gaze focused far away.*

*"Mother?" I questioned, reaching out for her as she swayed on her feet. I*

*was only twelve but already I was taller and larger than her. I helped her to a chair and got her a cup of tea as she sat, her eyes hazy. My mother was a Fae psychic, a powerful one. This wasn't unusual behavior for her, so I sat beside her and waited for her to come back.*

*"She will love you," her voice was husky. I frowned at her. She never spoke during her episodes. "And you her. She'll leave you. But she knows what she's doing. Trust her. She will know your heart. She's the only one who ever will. She is your other half, Fin. The anger, the hatred, you'll have for her—let it go."*

*I took her hand in mine and held it as her small body began to shake. I had no clue what she was talking about. She was babbling, her words coming out in strings of sentences that made no sense.*

*"You must save her for she will try to destroy herself over and over again. The night is dark. She hurts. She'll die without you. Go to her. Your heart and hers. They will be one. It is meant to be. She's troubled. She will push and pull you, tearing at you. It's a love that cannot be denied or controlled. You both will sacrifice so much for one another. Infinity. Forever."*

*She blinked rapidly, her eyes coming back into focus as she stared at me.*

*"Mother? What was that?" I asked, knowing damn well she was speaking to me. That I was meant to hear her words, even if those words didn't have a clear meaning. Everly's face surfaced in my mind, making me ill. I silently said a prayer that she was OK.*

*"You'll understand when you're older," she murmured, reaching out and cupping my face, a sad smile on her lips. "Promise you won't forget?"*

*"I promise," I answered, helping her to her feet.*

*"That's my Fin." She squeezed my hand. She was the only one to ever call me that. Whenever I asked her why, she'd always giggle, ruffle my hair, and tell me she knew I was meant for something great that would last more than a lifetime. Infinity. I was meant for forever.*

*"Please, fetch my cloak? I wish to pick flowers."*

*I quickly retrieved her cloak and placed it around her slender shoulders, moving her long blonde hair aside.*

*"You're going to be great." She took my hand in hers and held it tightly. "Brave. Strong. A good man. A fighter."*

"Mother, you're scaring me," I replied, continuing to frown. She wasn't acting like herself.

"Don't be afraid, sweetheart. Your strength will be one of your greatest attributes. You're meant to love someday. Be brave when it happens because it'll be such a force that it'll leave you breathless. You will know she's the one because she'll sing it for you."

"And if my heart and mind war over it?" I asked, gazing down at her.

"Then to the victor go the spoils," she chuckled sadly. "Now, come. It's getting late. I have a feeling this is the last time I'll go to pick flowers."

I walked with her out to her horse and helped her on, pushing her cryptic words out of my head. Then I climbed on mine, and we made our way out to the edge of the kingdom where she proceeded to pick flowers, humming a sad, sweet tune—one that she hummed whenever she was busy or thinking.

A warmness washed over me, the one that signaled Everly needed me. I jumped to my feet, sweat beading on my brow. My mother's head snapped in my direction, and she gave me a melancholy, knowing look.

"Go to her. I'll be here when you get back." She walked to me.

"Go home, mother. It's far too late to be out here. Please," I wheezed out, wiping at my brow as the pull grew stronger. "I'm getting a terrible feeling."

"Trust your instincts, Fin," she said, squeezing my hands. "What will happen is meant to happen. Know that. And know that I am so very proud of you. I always will be."

She came up on her toes and planted a tender kiss on my cheek.

"I love you, Fin. Now go. She needs you more than I do."

And so I went. I left her alone. She died because I went to save Everly. She was alone out there while I was cradling Everly in my arms. Then I returned and found her lifeless body lying beneath an oak tree, her daisies scattered and wilted on the ground around her.

Ever since her death, I'd blamed myself. I'd blamed my father. I'd blamed Everly. If I'd just made her go home… If I'd just stayed… But if I had, Everly would've been gone.

I shook my head bitterly. I hated vampires. So, I vowed to kill any who maliciously crossed my path. My mother would've forgiven her killer. I knew she'd want me to as well, but I couldn't. I wouldn't. And

I prayed someday I'd find the monster who took her from me. When I did, I'd make him suffer like he made her suffer. Like he made *me* suffer. My mother deserved to be avenged, and someday she would be as I plunged my blade through the heart of her killer.

# CHAPTER 9

"What did the Order say?" Eric knocked on my bedroom door and poked his head in. I didn't answer him. I was sitting at my desk staring out my window at the dark campus grounds below. "Shadow, come on, man. You've been holed up in your room for *two* days. You haven't even come out to eat. We figured we'd leave you alone for a few days, but tomorrow's day three. You're starting to worry us. Not to mention, Amara is driving me nuts. You know how much I can't stand her."

I'd been plagued with worry over what may very well be true. It was eating at me. I replayed the scene with my mother over and over in my head. Deep down I'd blamed Everly for my mother's death. But even harboring those thoughts, I couldn't stop longing to see her again. It angered me, making me sick to my stomach because I *knew* how much I hated her for drawing me to her. I couldn't stop the urge that was inside me to be near her, aching to be released. Just thinking she was out there without any protection made me grind my teeth. But at the same time, I wanted her gone. I didn't want to think about the girl I cared so much for it hurt. The same girl I hated so much it made me see red. The girl I blamed for keeping me away when my mother needed me. Even after all these years, that push and pull my mother spoke of tore at my mind, body, and soul.

I thought about what the Order said. I really didn't want to drag Everly into the Conexus, even though as the general I'd be in control of what she had to do. It was an honor to be part of it, sure, but it wasn't for her. My heart couldn't handle it. Bringing her to Dementon, the school my squad policed to ensure the safety of all the students, was my main concern. I knew if she was here, she wouldn't be in danger, and if by chance something happened, at least I'd be near her. The thought of seeing her all the time made my stomach clench painfully. The Cipher and the creatures from the void wouldn't be able to get to her here though. And *that* trumped all. The dead would be another issue, but I knew they'd have to be brave or stupid to wander onto Dementon grounds. Recently, Sangrey found a way for us to capture the wandering dead—through a voidbox, a device that could house a spirt and send it to Xanan to be kept in a holding area lined with vorbex, a deep purple, crystal-like gem used to house the wandering dead and other dark creatures. I'd never asked what happened to them once they were in the holding area. Past me sending them there, I didn't care.

*Why* I cared so much about anything Ever-related made me angry. I didn't want this. I didn't when I was four, and I sure as hell didn't now. The whole ordeal had killed my mother.

And then there was Amara. I'd been avoiding her like the plague. I knew she and I needed to talk.

"Where's Damien?" I asked softly, not bothering to look at him. Eric stepped into the room.

"He's downstairs trying to get Sloane to make out with him. He's failing, by the way. She's already turned him into a frog, but he's a shifter so he just shifted back."

"Get him. Meet me at Dice Road. The cemetery. Midnight."

"We doing a hunt?" Eric asked, brightening up.

"Something like that," I murmured, casting him a quick glance.

Sensing my seriousness, Eric nodded and left my room. I was tugging my cloak on when there was a soft knock on the door.

"Who is it?" I asked, pausing as I put my long dark cape on over my black hunting gear.

"It's me. Amara."

"Shit," I grumbled. I didn't feel like dealing with her, but it was inevitable. We hadn't said two words to one another since our argument on the campus grounds. "Come in," I called out. She came into the room wearing her black uniform, her red hair cascading down her shoulders. My gaze roved over each of her features. Still no butterflies.

"Eric said you're going on a mission. I wanted to know if you needed any help."

"Did Eric tell you I needed help?" I asked, raising an eyebrow at her and adjusting my cloak on my shoulders.

"No."

"Then I think you know the answer," I pointed out evenly. She was silent as her eyes raked over me, her lower lip trembling.

"I don't want to fight with you. I just want to be involved."

"You are involved by staying out of my way while I do my job," I sighed, grabbing my leather gloves and slipping them on. I went to the small weapons rack in my room where I liked to keep a few things and took my blades down and began fastening them to me.

"I worry about you—"

"Don't," I snapped. "I can take care of myself, Amara. You *know* that."

"You've been hiding out in your room for days now. What did the Order tell you?"

"That I have to do this mission."

"And?"

"And? I'm sure you already know." I shook my head, my silver hair falling forward. I quickly grabbed a rubber band and pulled my hair away from my face and stared pointedly at her.

"My father mentioned it. Are you mad?" She took a step to me, her eyes traveling over my face.

"I'm furious, Amara! How long have you known?" I demanded, folding my arms over my chest. "And why wouldn't you tell me?"

"I only just found out! I swear it!" She came to me and wrapped her arms around my body in a hug. "Would it be so bad? To be married to me?

"Amara, you know how I feel! Why would you think an arranged marriage would make me feel any better? Huh? This is not how you make a relationship work. If I wanted to marry you, I'd ask you, and I sure as hell wouldn't be doing it right now! We're too young for God's sake!"

"We don't have to if you don't want to." She hugged me tighter. I let out a sigh and gave her a small, one-armed squeeze. It was the best I could muster under my current mental condition.

"I don't," I said softly, firmly. She shook against me before looking up at me with bright eyes, the tears glistening in them.

"I know," she said sadly. "But my heart says that maybe someday you will. We've been together for a long time. That has to mean something to you. It does to me."

Not wanting to continue the conversation any further, I leaned down and silenced her with a kiss. She eagerly accepted it, her tongue sweeping along mine. I wasn't sure what the hell I was doing, but I did it anyway, dragging her to my bed, wanting everything plaguing me to just go away.

I just wanted to be me again.

*I* tugged my shirt back over my head, feeling like a total jerk. I never stuck around afterwards. She knew that though. It was just one of the many things that made me wonder why she bothered being my girlfriend.

"When will you be back?" she asked, sheets wrapped around her in my bed.

"I don't know," I grunted, feeling sick for being with her when I had all these mixed feelings going on in my head. The last thing I wanted was to lead her on. I hated myself for it.

"Is it that girl?" she ventured, sliding to the edge of my bed.

"Yes," I muttered hurriedly, shoving a blade into my holster that had fallen out when I'd taken off my pants. "And if you tell anyone about this, you'll be punished in Xanan. It's a serious offense to give away secret mission information once I've given it out to members. I am the *only* one who knows about all missions and who has the power to share that information with everyone. Do *not* share with anyone what I've told you. Eric and Damien are the only two who know."

"I know." She pouted, reaching out for me. "I understand. I really am just worried about you. This isn't normal. You have to know that. This girl—she could be crazy. She could hurt you."

I stared down at her as she got to her feet and looked at me. She reached up and pushed my silver-gray hair off my forehead. While rolling around in my bed, some of the strands had fallen from the rubber band. Tilting her chin up, her lips met mine. I wasn't sure what I was doing anymore... what I was feeling. Desperation. Agony. Confusion. I kissed her back. I kissed her pretending she was Everly, the girl my heart both loathed and loved. Just like I'd crawled into bed and buried myself in her moments ago imaging she was Everly. It was wrong, but the thought of my lips on Everly's made the dam inside of me burst open, the swell of emotion pouring out of me onto Amara's lips. She let out a soft moan, her fingers tangling in my shaggy hair.

I got my wits about me and pulled away leaving her to whimper at my distance.

"I have to go. Go to bed."

"Will you come see me when you get back?" she asked coyly. "I'll wait for you."

"No." I looked her up and down, knowing I'd made a huge mistake taking her to bed. Foolishly, I'd hoped the butterflies would beat their wings again. Well, the nauseous twinges that I hoped would one day metamorphose into butterflies. But nothing. I was empty inside. "Just go to bed. *Your* bed."

Her fingers pressed against her lips. "You never kiss me like that. I know you're having trouble with your feelings. I'll wait. You know I will."

"*Don't* wait for me, Amara. I'm not that guy. We both know that." I melded into the shadows and disappeared into the darkness not waiting for her answer.

# CHAPTER 10

"*an*, why did we have to meet here?" Damien grumbled as he appeared beside me with Eric in the middle of the dark cemetery.

"It was the best place," I murmured, walking forward through the tombstones, still feeling sick over my night with Amara. Inwardly, I rolled my eyes. It's not like we'd never done *it* before. We had plenty of times since we'd started dating. But it shouldn't have happened tonight, especially with how messed up my head was. I hated myself for it and vowed not to do it again until I had my shit sorted.

"They say this place is stupid haunted." Eric shivered, looking around. "I can feel *them*."

"Me too," Damien muttered. "Can we walk faster please?"

"Wusses," I sighed, breaking into a trot. Conexus typically didn't mess with the dead unless they were haunting a place or causing issues. Then we went in and took them out, or rather, captured them and sent them to Xanan. I didn't have much information on what happened past that since no one was really able to see or speak to them. My guess was the Order was working on a way to use them to their advantage against the Cipher. The idea that Ever might be able to *help* them made me nauseous. But if it would end the Cipher threat, it might not be a bad idea. It just wasn't an idea I wanted to explore right then.

We reached the edge of the cemetery gates and stopped.

"So, what are we doing here?" Eric asked, his form completely black, his eyes a dull orangish red. His form matched mine and Damien's.

"I want to show you something. Follow me and remain quiet. No matter what. We'll communicate telepathically if we must." Communicating telepathically was a gift members of Conexus got once inducted. It was one of Eric's main abilities and was therefore something we all could share, just like my shadow melding and Damien's strength. Each member provided an enhancement. To be paired off with someone was stellar because everything the two connecting members had would become enhanced. Eric's telepathy proved quite helpful in battle and instances like this—not that there were many—but it had its limits. We needed to be near one another, and it only worked with other members. When Specials were inducted into Conexus, one of their gifts would enhance the rest of us. That's why I was picky when choosing. I wanted the best.

I led them down the darkened street and walked straight up to Everly's door.

"You brought us to your side chick's house?" Damien chuckled. "Nice touch, Shadow. I'm rubbing off on you."

"Shut it, Wick." I tossed him a sour look which only made him laugh more.

"I swear if you've brought us here to witness you kill this girl you're going to have a really tough time," Eric warned me.

Sighing, I shook my head and pressed my hand to the door. It glowed momentarily before I moved my hand away. Placing my hands on each of my friends' shoulders, I brought us outside of Everly's bedroom door.

"What the hell—" Damien started, clearly surprised at the talent I'd just shown him, but I shook my head at him, reminding him to be quiet. He gave me a curt nod. Her door was cracked open, so we were able to step inside her bedroom. She was lying in her bed, her long black hair a tangled mess around her. My throat was tight as I stopped and peered down at her, all sorts of emotions rushing through me.

God, she was beautiful. Her plump, pink lips were slightly parted. Her chest moved deeply as she breathed. Long, dark lashes fanned across her ivory cheeks. Blankets were tangled around her toned legs, revealing her tiny pink shorts riding high on her thighs. A patch of her perfect tummy was visible as her small white tank crept up her torso.

*"This is her?"* Eric's voice was in my mind. I nodded, unable to yank my eyes away from her.

*"Damn. No wonder you've gone temporarily stupid. I'm feeling a little dumb myself right now,"* Damien's voice cut in. *"God, she's freaking gorgeous. When I asked you if she was hot, you didn't say anything. I assumed she was a troll and you were embarrassed."*

He reached out to touch her hair, but I slapped his hand away.

*"Don't touch her,"* I growled at him, my protectiveness over her kicking in.

*"Damn, dude, chill. Her hair looks soft. I just wanted to check. I wasn't going to hurt her!"*

She shifted as she slept, her shirt creeping up dangerously high. I reached down and tugged it gently back into place. Her eyelids fluttered, her breath quickening.

*"She's dreaming,"* Eric mused. *"I wonder what about."*

We didn't have to wait long to find out.

"Shadow," she said softly. My name on her lips sent a thrill of excitement through me. I'd never told her my name, or rather, my nickname. It was an interesting development. "Help me. Please." She gave a tiny whimper, her eyebrows crinkling.

"I'm here," I murmured without thinking. I sat on the edge of her bed and pushed her long hair off her forehead tenderly. She nuzzled her face into my hand, her lips brushing against it as she moved her head. My heart quickened in my chest. I closed my eyes, not wanting to feel this way for her. It felt... *wrong*. My mother was gone because of my draw to her. I couldn't help myself. I was a victim to something greater. Something I didn't want to consider, so I continued to cradle her face tenderly, watching as her eyelids fluttered with whatever dream plagued her to the point of calling out for me.

*"Should we leave you two alone?"* Damien asked coyly.

*"Shut up, Damien. Will you be OK with her?"* Eric's voice sounded off, weird, in my mind.

*"Yes,"* I replied softly. *"I won't hurt her."*

*"You better not,"* Eric stated darkly. *"We'll be outside in her hallway, lurking in the dark like a couple weirdos. Come on."* Eric tugged Damien away and slid through her open door.

I ignored them as I sat and watched her for what felt like forever, and yet even that wasn't long enough. I could gaze at this girl for an eternity, and my heart would still crave more. I swallowed hard at the realization.

"Save me," she whimpered. "Please. Don't let me go," her voice was garbled with sleep, her brows crinkled tightly. A tear slid from the corner of her eye. I gently wiped the tear away as I leaned into her.

"I'll never let you go, Everly. As much as I know I should. As much as I want to. I'll always save you even if it kills me to do it." I pressed a gentle kiss to her forehead. Her brows unfused, and she stopped fidgeting as her breathing became deep and even again. I'd never had so many butterflies hammering a rhythm in my guts or chest before. Being near her caused my heart to beat rapidly. The feeling was totally unique and foreign, but somehow, something I didn't want to end.

I didn't want to leave her, but I had to. I had to tell the guys what was going on.

What I might be. What Everly might be. Fighting it wasn't going to change the possibility.

And I *hated* it. I hated being forced into this. I hated Everly being forced into it. I hated my mother being gone. I hated caring for Everly one minute and then hating her the next. I hated myself for the way I felt. I was just a giant ball of anger and hatred.

It was time I started to come to terms with what it might mean for all of us.

# CHAPTER 11

"She's hot, dude," Damien said as we left her house. "I figured you must have been holding out information. She's hotter than Amara even. And that's saying something."

"Don't talk about her like that," I said, stepping off her front step.

"Who, Amara?" Damien asked.

"No. Everly."

"Wait. I'm confused. What's really happening here?" Damien dragged me to a stop. "You're *with* Amara. What's the deal with this girl? A few days ago you were plotting to kill her. What's changed?"

"I don't know," I sighed, shaking my head. All my thoughts were twisted and muddled. "Nothing's changed, and yet everything has. I can't even explain it."

"Well, you should probably try because you have us confused," Damien continued. "Or at least give us an idea about your plans. Because I have to tell you, man, if you're too confused to figure it out, I definitely don't mind stepping in and taking care of her. I could introduce myself to her. Show her a good time while you try to figure things out—"

"You'll have no relationship with her," I growled, fisting my hand in his shirt collar and pulling him roughly to me. The very idea of someone touching her sent me into a bout of rage.

"Whoa, man. Chill." He held his hands up in surrender. I released him and ran a shaking hand over my face in frustration. *Damn. Why was she having this effect on me?* It was unsettling.

"Shadow, man. Talk to us. What's going on. This girl isn't even *your* girl. Why so protective?" Eric cut in. "Damien's right. You wanted her dead just a few days ago."

"She really *is* mine," I murmured, feeling faint.

Damien and Eric glanced at one another.

"Does *she* know it?" Damien ventured carefully as I looked up to her darkened bedroom window.

"I think subconsciously she knows it. Or at least she's close to realizing it," I sighed, wishing I could just go up to her room and take her small body into my arms and hold her forever. It was a terrible tugging in my core, one I had to wrestle with and kick into submission.

"Man, you're acting all sorts of crazy." Damien cleared his throat. "Does *Amara* know about all this? I know you said you weren't going to say anything, but you're acting weird."

"She doesn't know everything." I forced my gaze from her window and focused my red eyes on Damien. "I don't know what I'm doing. You're right. I wanted her dead. I still do, but the part that wants her to live is stronger. My brain is screwed up. My heart is at war with it. I don't feel for Amara what I feel with Everly. Not even close."

"Yeah, but Sleeping Beauty doesn't even know who you are," Eric's voice of reason broke in. "So, I think you need to take a step back and evaluate what the hell you're doing here. Being with a girl outside of Dementon is hard. Plus, you can't decide if you want to kill her or not? And can you imagine what your *father* would do if he found you dating outside your social class? And a Nattie?" Eric shuddered.

"She's not a Nattie," I replied. I drew in a deep breath before launching into what I'd been told by the Order. When I finished, Damien and Eric stared at me wide-eyed.

"Dude. No freaking way." Damien shook his head. "You? The

Reever? Her? The Mancer? What the hell are you going to do if it's true? You acted like we were crazy when we mentioned it!"

"Hopefully we never have to find out," I mumbled. "But I'm going to figure out how to get her to Dementon, so I can watch over her."

"Amara will *love* that." Eric rolled his eyes.

"Amara won't have a choice."

"So what are you going to do? Break it off with Amara and attempt something with this chick?" Eric asked, nodding in the direction of Everly's house.

"No." I shook my head. "I can never be with Everly, no matter h-how I end up feeling. It just can't be. I'll always blame her for my mother's death. Instead, I just want her to learn about herself. And prove me wrong. Convince me that maybe she deserves to live."

"See?" Damien shoved Eric in the shoulder. "You thought our boy was going to drop Amara, who puts out all the time, to chill with some chick who *might* talk to him? You're nuts. Amara is a pain in the ass, but he'd be nuts to let her go, especially if this chick doesn't even know what the hell she is. And she's not Conexus. It couldn't happen. Plus, the dead? Really? To hell with that. I couldn't deal with it. It's bad enough we have to capture the lost ones." Damien shuddered as he looked up to her bedroom window, backtracking on what he'd said earlier about trying to have a relationship with her.

"Look, we're going to watch over her. We're going to keep her safe. It's our new mission. And we tell *no one* about this. Got it? Everly is a secret. If she *is* who the Order thinks she is, she's going to need to be protected. If the Cipher get wind of this, she'll be in danger. She's in danger now. I mean, someone sent a wraith after her. She needs us," I finished.

"You know we have your back." Eric gave me a bro handshake. "Anything, man."

"Yeah, we got you," Damien added, shaking my hand like Eric did.

"I knew I could count on you guys." I grinned, feeling a bit better.

# CHAPTER 12

*I* was out on a haunt with Brandon, Sloane, Amanda, Adam, and Eric. My brow was wet with sweat, and I was unable to focus because I was worried about Everly. There was a nasty, nagging feeling in my guts. The pull. I'd been fighting it since I'd learned what it was. I couldn't—wouldn't—go to her. By focusing on it, I was able to control it a bit more. Damien had gone to watch over her. He had strict orders to remain unseen. He'd never failed me before. It wasn't him that was getting to me. There was this overwhelming feeling that something was *wrong* with her. Damien swore he'd fire message me if something happened. I knew I'd know before the message got to me though.

"I don't understand why we're trying to round up the dead," Sloane muttered as we walked into the abandoned old house. "Like I freaking hate this job so much. I didn't ask for this crap."

"No one usually does," Brandon murmured, his brown curls a mess on his head, his hazel eyes keen as he peered through the darkness. "I can feel them."

"Me too," Eric added. "There aren't many though." He took out the voidbox. It went straight to Xanan. It was a top-secret mission we'd acquired only weeks before. We were under tight orders to not speak of it to anyone at Xanan or with the council unless directly spoken to of it with the passcodes we were given. I didn't even know who'd handed the order down.

"Let's get this over with," I growled, drawing my blade.

"Why didn't Damien have to come?" Adam muttered. "Is he back home banging some Conexus groupie or something? Not fair, dude."

"No. Damien's on a mission," I replied, stepping forward. "And he'll be getting back at daybreak, around the same time as us. So, let's cut the crap and get going."

They all followed me up the rickety old stairs to the first room on the left. We could sense them in there. I felt them just a little bit more, their outlines shifting in and out of my vision through the closed door. My dead-vision had been getting better since Everly had drawn me to her. I tried to push away the nagging idea that she was the mancer, and our gifts were just getting stronger with one another.

I kicked the door open and darted into the room. In the center stood a wraith twice my height, and that was saying something since I was a tall dude.

"Ahh, I can ssssmell you, Conexusss," the wraith hissed. Its hollow black sockets dripped a black fluid while its gnarled body twisted and jerked with each movement. A jagged row of sharp teeth laden with a putrid smelling fluid flashed as it spoke.

"Piss off," I growled, whipping my sword at it. The creature knocked my sword aside as it soared through the air. A moment later, we were surrounded by two more wraiths and at least six of the lost ones.

"Great," Brandon shivered, pulling out his voidbox. Sloane mimicked him, a frown on her pretty face. No one liked haunts. I let my group do their thing, keeping my focus on the wraith in front of me.

"I know what you areee," the wraith hissed out in an almost sing-song voice.

"You don't know shit," I spat at it as we circled one another.

"Reveeeeerrrr." It laughed hoarsely, making my blood freeze in my veins. "We're coming for her, fool boy. She'll die soon."

"What are you talking about?" I snarled at it as we continued to move around one another.

"It's what he wantsss. He has seennn it, you seeee. He sendsss usss to collect her when she fallsss. And ssshe will fall. And he will catch her when she doesss."

"*Who?* Who will catch her? The *Overlord?*" I demanded, thinking of the vampire overlord, Aviram, the head of the Cipher.

"Ssstupid boy!" The creature cackled. "You are blinded by your titlesss. He comesss for her. Soon!"

I'd had enough. I lunged forward and jammed my knife through its empty eye-socket. It let out a terrible squeal, and I pressed my palm to its forehead. Understanding dawned on me in that instant. I wasn't like the other members. I didn't need a voidbox. I knew in that moment the creature would go to the same place the rest of them were going. It withered and popped before it disappeared, leaving its stench behind.

"Damn." Eric patted me on the shoulder. "You get a new ability every single mission, man. You're going to be all-powerful before long."

I didn't say anything at his words. We had to get these nests taken care of. I needed a report from Damien. The creature's words were on repeat in my head. Everly was in danger. He'd confirmed it. And wraiths couldn't lie. Not really. They typically spoke in riddles or in circles, never giving an answer, always creating more questions. But *never* lies.

We ended up powering through a slew of nests that night, collecting over a hundred lost ones and a wraith here and there.

"You do realize we collected more wraiths tonight than we have in the last year?" Amanda, one of our shifters, pointed out as we stood outside the grounds to Dementon. "Don't you find that odd?" She cast a quick look at me with her dark eyes. She was right.

"Yeah," I grunted, looking down at my watch. Damien should be back any time now. His long seventy-two hours were almost up. I was needed to tear nests and haunts apart, and Eric was needed for his stitch ability. The only hitch with his ability was that he needed to be right in the center of whatever he was stopping, and it seriously drained him. Damien had no choice but to take a long shift. "There's been a surge in them. The Order thinks it's Cipher related."

"Wouldn't surprise me." Brandon yawned and wiped at his sweaty brow. "They've been wanting to take over the Order for years. Guess they'll go to any measure to do it."

"They'll never win." Eric shrugged. "But they're welcome to try."

"Yeah, because we have the best general ever." Adam grinned at me. I returned his smile with my own quick one.

"I just wished we didn't have to do this *every* single night. There are times when I'd like to kick back and just watch a movie," Chloe sighed.

"Where's the fun in that, Chloe?" Brandon chuckled. She grinned back at him.

"You guys ready to go back?" I asked.

"Do we have to?" Sloane whined. "Can't we just go get a Nattie breakfast in a diner or something? I get so annoyed being so uppity on the grounds. I miss my friends."

"We're your friends," Eric pointed out.

"I'm talking about Harper and Abby." She pouted, referring to her old caster friends. I rolled my eyes and pushed off the wall I was leaning against.

"We're going back. Get ready," I said, pressing my hand against the Dementon seal of a lion on the gateway. It glowed red before the heavy metal doors swung open. Sloane stepped through with only a few minor complaints. Once the gates shut behind us, we squinted our eyes as the Dementon grounds came into view.

"Where are you going in such a hurry?" Brandon called out to me as I broke into a jog.

"Damien," I shouted over my shoulder, running to our dorms now full tilt, which was insanely fast.

I had to get his report. I was so sick I thought I was going to lose it.

# CHAPTER 13

"*D*amn, dude. Relax," Damien rubbed his eyes as I burst into our commons and grabbed him by the shirt, tugging him to my office. Amara stood up to come to me, but I gave her a quick shake of my head. I was so not in the mood to deal with her. Jared looked interestedly at us but didn't make to move. He went back to watching the television.

"What's going on? I *felt* her all day and night. She's upset or sick or something," I demanded, the moment I slammed my door closed.

"Well…" Damien sank down into a chair across from my desk and yawned. "She has boyfriend troubles."

I bristled at the news, my heart sinking. A *boyfriend*. Of course, she had to have one.

"I mean, ex-boyfriend. She broke up with him. From my under-standing, he cheated on her with some chick named Britney. He tried getting back with her, and she turned him down. But she's hurting. She's sad. She masks her feelings. But she's actually really funny. Beautiful smile. Great rack—"

"Damien," I warned, growling.

"Sorry. She doesn't have many friends. She doesn't talk to a lot of people. The guys all want her, though. You should hear the shit they say about her. I doubt any of it's true."

"What do they say?" I asked, pacing the room.

"Well, I'm guessing she doesn't put out and that's what led to her breakup with this Dylan character. He came to her asking her to get back with him and she rejected him. She cried a little that night. Then they all started saying crap about how she begged him to take her back, how she tried to put out, but *he* turned her down. You know, typical lame-ass high school rumors."

"Is she OK?" I asked, stopping to stare at him, surprising myself with the passion of the question.

"I think so." He narrowed his eyes at me, taking me in like I had three heads or something. I knew what he was thinking just by the look on his face. "She's quiet, man. She reads a lot. She isn't big on talking. She has a friend named Nina who tries to get her to open up. She's a tough nut to crack. Just for the record, her friend is also hot."

"So no wraiths or lost ones?" I asked, ignoring his talk about her friend.

"Nothing. All was quiet. She slept like an angel. Said your name a few times in her sleep. I slept on the floor by her closet, which was creepy. I could've sworn I heard them scraping around inside there."

"Probably." I nodded. "They used to come through her closet."

"Wish I'd have known that before." Damien grimaced and gave a shudder. "Maintaining shadow is tiring, and my body feels weird. I need a shower and my bed." He rose from his seat and came to my side and patted me on the shoulder. "We good?"

"Was she really OK? She didn't cry much, right?" I asked, not meeting his eyes.

"She's strong. A few tears fell, but she wiped them away like a champ and kept moving on. That guy wants her, though. *Bad.* I peeked in on him. He's taking their breakup hard, considering he's the one who screwed up. She's a good girl, man. You know what I said about Amara and you keeping her around?"

I nodded.

"Forget I said that. Make yourself known to Everly. I think you two would be good for one another. And believe it or not, I'm pretty sure she already loves you, and if she doesn't, she's damn close. So, you know, don't kill her."

I didn't say anything as he left the room. I had to see her. It was my watch anyway. I hastily showered and melded from my bedroom to avoid talking to Amara.

When I got to Everly's room, she was just getting ready for school. I hadn't really dropped in on her like that before. I stuck to the shadows, creating them as I needed to, subtle darknesses here and there. From behind her, I watched in the mirror as she applied her pink lip gloss. Her brilliant green eyes were sad. Her dark hair was up in a high ponytail. It still reached the middle of her back. She was beautiful in her low-slung jeans, band t-shirt, and black chucks.

Grabbing her bag, she slung it over her shoulder and went downstairs and out the front door. I followed along, watching as she walked quickly, making sure nothing was out to harm her. She seemed to have a decent day at school. I stuck as close to her as I could. Damien was right—the girls in her group didn't seem to like her. It was probably because she was so much prettier than them. She was intimidating without trying. Only her friend Nina seemed to be genuine.

Annoyance simmered in my gut as Dylan stared at her from across the halls and crowded lunchroom. Deciding I had to see what he was up to, I made my way to his group.

"You need to let it go. She told you to piss off," a blond guy said, nudging Dylan as he gazed at Everly picking at her salad.

"I can't let it go. I screwed up. I have to make it right, Jax. I need her to know how sorry I am."

"Why?" Jax snorted, following his eyes to where Everly sat. "If you were really sorry, you wouldn't still be banging Britney. I say you deserve everything she's giving you."

"What am I going to do? She won't even look at me."

"Dude, she hates you. And for good reason—"

"I'm going to get her back. She's my girl. At your party. I'm sure Nina will make her go. I'll talk to her then. I'll tell her I love her—"

"You already did that," Jax pointed out.

"She was mad then. It's been a few days. She's had time to cool off," Dylan reasoned.

"Dude, there's a rumor going around that she begged you to take her back, and you told her no. And that's the *nice* rumor circulating. She's hurting. Just leave her be for now. Give her some time."

"No." Dylan shook his head firmly. "Do you know how many other dudes want to get in her pants? Ever is a hot commodity in this place. A virgin. Gorgeous. She's mine. All that shit is mine. I'll be the first. I'm going to make it happen."

"You're nuts," Jax snorted. I had to back away before I popped into existence and floored the douche. I went back to Everly and folded my arms over my chest as I watched her. She gave a half-hearted grin to Nina before her eyes traveled to where Dylan was. My heart clenched.

"Don't even think about it, Everly," I growled as this insane jealous rage took over me. I nearly became visible, my form shaking as I began to lose control. I had to go. I cast her one last look before melding back to Dementon.

I kicked open the front door to our commons, angrier than I'd ever been in my entire life, and more determined than ever before to keep *my* Everly safe, even from herself.

# CHAPTER 14

*I* couldn't go back to her, so I slept on it. For *days*. I sent Eric instead. He and Damien swapped back and forth as I continued to deal with Order garbage and my own sanity. I was sitting in my office, worrying about her, when Eric suddenly appeared.

"What?" I demanded, getting to my feet.

"She's going to a party. The one you said the friend was having. This guy wants her. I think you need to go."

I didn't need to be told twice. Without thought, I melded straight to her room, wondering why the hell I was doing this to myself. My breath froze in my lungs as she walked out of her bathroom looking unbelievably gorgeous in her jean skirt and black top. She went to her vanity and leaned forward, putting her lip gloss on. And that was when I lost it. I shimmered into view as a shadow, desperately wanting to speak to her.

She froze, her pretty eyes locked on my red ones through the mirror.

"W-who are you?" she asked, her voice shaking. I couldn't answer her. I was tongue-tied. Besides, I knew I shouldn't. Instead, I willed myself to disappear, traveling straight out of her house to the sidewalk. In the fresh air, I drew in a few deep breaths and watched as she rushed outside, her eyes traveling back to her house fearfully.

*Great. I'd scared her.*

Nina waited in her car for Everly to climb inside. Once the door shut, Nina sped off. If I couldn't hold it together just looking at her, I sure as hell wouldn't be able to if that douche came around her.

So, I made my way back to Dementon and found Eric and Damien relaxing in the commons.

"I need you guys to go to her," I said quietly as I entered the room.

"What's wrong?" Eric asked as they both followed me to my office.

"I-I lost control and showed my shadow-self to her. I scared her. I can't be there. I need you guys to do this. If I even hear that guy breathe, I'll lose my shit."

"We'll go." Eric nodded. "But you need to talk to Amara. She's been asking us questions all night."

"OK" I sighed, knowing I needed to talk to her. I still feared our parents would arrange a marriage that I knew I damn well didn't want. I'd been putting off the dreaded breakup conversations for reasons I didn't grasp.

"Alright. Come on, man." Damien melded, and Eric followed suit. A sigh of relief escaped my lips. I needed a shower and a nap, in that order. Then, I'd talk to Amara.

# CHAPTER 15

Gasping, I was jolted from my sleep by panic. Anger. Confusion. I sat up, the feeling gnawing at my guts. Then blinding pain overwhelmed me. I fell to the floor, gasping, crawling on my hands and knees.

"Shadow!" Damien burst into my bedroom and rushed to me. "It's her. It's Everly! We tried to get there, but we weren't fast enough!"

"W-what happened?" I gasped, my body spasming painfully.

"A car. It-it struck her. I-I think she's dying. Eric stayed behind. We need to get you there! She needs you!" I reached out to him, and he tugged me to my feet. Instantly, we melded to a dark road. I let out a shuddering gasp, lurching forward on the edge of the scene, trying to draw in calming breaths and get my head together so I could help her. I didn't even need to think twice about it. I'd gone from wanting her dead to needing her to live. She *had* to prove me wrong. I needed her to. I needed her to show me she was more than the girl I blamed for my mother's death. I wanted her to be great. To be worth the sacrifice.

I breathed in deeply, painfully, and narrowed my eyes as I surveyed what was happening.

When I saw all the blood pooling around her broken body, a cry erupted from deep inside of me. Her body was spasming, twitching, on the pavement. Dylan clutched her hand and cried over her. Suddenly, I wished I'd had killed her that first night I came back just so she wouldn't be suffering in that moment.

"I'm so sorry!" he called out. "Don't die, Ever!"

"I tried stitching. It's not working," Eric said desperately, his blue glow fading away.

I shoved him and Damien away from me and went to her with steady steps, pushing the pain away. Looming over her, I cocked my head as I took in the scene.

Dear God. There was *so* much blood. She was going to die.

I fell to my knees and reached my hand out to her, my mother's words slamming into me.

*"The night is dark. She hurts. She'll die without you. Go to her. Your heart and hers. They will be one. It is meant to be."*

Her pretty green eyes wavered, glassy, before she reached out for me, the creature no one else could see. Dylan was too busy begging her to breathe to pay any attention to anything she was doing.

I wrapped my hand firmly around hers, feeling her energy fall away from her. She wasn't going to last long. Maybe ten minutes at the most. Blood dribbled from her mouth, and her body shook as she tried to breathe. She was dying. And she was in so much pain. I could feel it.

I focused everything I had on her.

"Breathe," I commanded her, my voice distorted through shadow. "I'll do the rest." I didn't even know if it would work, but I was damn well willing to try.

Her small body wracked with another tremor as she tried to obey me, her eyes wild and scared.

"Everly!" I shouted at her frantically, losing myself for a moment and shimmering. "Don't stop! Focus on me. Stay with me. No matter what, don't stop."

*"My heart,"* she sputtered out in my mind, startling me. *How was she in my head? She wasn't Conexus.* Her heart thumped unevenly, slowly, fading away, the beats few and far between.

"It's not beating like it should," I answered, my heart breaking as I stared at her scared face, her eyes fixed on me, silently begging me to help her. In the past, I'd always helped her. I couldn't let her down now. All my terrible thoughts from earlier vanished. It was her. And me. Like always.

*"Am I dead?"* her voice was in my head again.

"Not yet," my voice was still distorted from the depths of the shadows. "Your heart barely beats, but you still live. Do you *want* to die?" My voice cracked with the words, hoping she chose the easiest answer for both of us. What that answer was, I didn't know, but both choices broke my heart for different reasons.

*"I-no,"* she whimpered, her body trembling. *"I-I want to live."*

"You will not be the same. You're special." I couldn't lie to her. She had to know everything I could possibly warn her about. "Who you were will die tonight on this pavement, and a new you will be reborn from the ashes and misery. Death stalks you tonight." My eyes swept over her face before I gave a shudder and closed my eyes. I was going to try this. I *had* to. I was about to alter our destinies if everything was true. *Forever.* But she was worth it. She had to be. I prayed she was. I'd keep her safe. I'd promised, and this was me keeping that promise. "Do you accept what this could mean for you? Do you understand that nothing will ever be the same? Because Ever, you're going to die here tonight, whether you continue to breathe or not."

*"I'm afraid."* She wept, tears leaking from her emerald green eyes. A strange look swept over her face. I *knew* that look. She was going to leave me. No. *No!*

"Fight it," I commanded her in a deep voice. "It will be *my* battle, not yours. I will take it all away. Trust me, Everly. I won't hurt you. I would never hurt you," my voice cracked on the last sentence. I was such a liar!

"Who *are* you?" she gasped out, her body spasming again.

"Tonight, I'm your lucky penny," I breathed out. I placed my free hand over her heart. Working on instinct alone with my mother's words about our hearts echoing in my mind, I felt my energy begin to transfer to her, giving her a bit of healing. Some of her wounds mended. But her injuries were extensive. She'd have to fight many of them on her own. I just had to take enough away to save her. The more I took from her, the more pain engulfed me. Still I continued taking everything I could from her, so she wouldn't suffer.

"Are you an angel?" she choked out.

"Definitely not an angel," I answered sadly, painfully. "I'm your only hope—your last hope. This will change everything, and for that I *am* sorry. If you want this, if you want life and what this moment means, then breathe for me, Ever. Don't stop once you start. I'll be weakened until you awaken and won't be able to help you." If it was anything like Eric's and everyone else's best abilities, it would take me time to recover.

Her eyes locked on mine as she drew in breath after breath, fighting the battle along with me. She *was* a good girl. We needed one another. I kept my eyes locked on hers, letting her know that I was there for her. With her.

"Breathe," I murmured fiercely. My hand on her chest trembled violently, the last bit of energy I had left going into her. Her heart began to thud normally while mine quaked and stumbled in my chest. "Keep breathing, Everly. Breathe for me," I wheezed out, trying to sound strong for her.

"Who are you?" she called out again in my mind.

"I-I am everything we both fear," I answered painfully, everything hitting me all at once. Everything she saw moments before her near-death collided with me, pain and all. Along the edge of the dark street, I thought I saw movement. Perhaps a wraith. I couldn't be sure because everything was hazy and painful. It was probably just my imagination. I prayed it was.

I crumpled to the ground beside her, unable to withstand the agony I was in. I knew in my mind that it was true. I was the Reever, and she was the Mancer.

And together, we'd be unstoppable.

# CHAPTER 16

*I* hurt. *Bad.* I hurt in places I didn't think I could ever hurt. Even breathing was a painful ordeal. My ribs and lungs screamed at me with every short breath I tried to rake in. The underside of my wrist burned and itched. Absentmindedly, I rubbed it.

"Shit," I groaned painfully, opening my eyes.

"He's awake! Get Brandon!" Eric shouted out. There was a rush of footsteps as someone retreated from my room. My room. I was back in the Conexus house.

"God," I moaned, struggling as I sat up. My bones were on fire, and my head felt like a marching band had just swept through it leaving behind a dull roar in its wake. "Where's Everly? Is she OK?" I was frantic and bleary-eyed as I struggled to get out of bed. All I knew was that I had to make sure she was safe. A set of strong hands started to push me back in bed, but I shoved them away.

"Dude, lie down! Brandon is on his way! You aren't strong enough yet!" Eric shouted. I didn't care. I *needed* to see her. Needed to make sure she was OK. I fell to the floor and began crawling to my door. I wasn't strong enough to meld, but I'd sure as hell crawl there on my hands and knees if I had to.

"Shadow, please," Amara called out helplessly. "*Stop*. Eric, do something! He's going to hurt himself again!"

Eric reached out for me, but I pushed him off again. A moment later Damien and Brandon entered. They immediately swooped down and hauled my weak body back to my bed.

"Get the hell off me!" I snarled, struggling to break free.

"Why is he acting like this?" Amara demanded. "Brandon, fix it!"

"I'm trying," Brandon growled, placing his hands on either side of my face. Warmth flowed through me, relaxation following. Brandon could simmer down emotions. Damn him for doing it to me.

"Knock it off, Rice," I snapped at him. He released me and gave me a sheepish smile and a shrug.

"Where's Everly?" I demanded, not hurting nearly as much as I had been moments before. "Is she OK? Someone tell me!"

"She's in the hospital," Damien broke in. "I was there this morning."

"And?"

"And..." Damien looked around the room at everyone. "I think we should speak alone."

"I'm *not* leaving!" Amara folded her arms over her chest. "He's my boyfriend. And he almost *died*! And for some girl no one knows! I want to hear what's going on—"

"Amara, this is a private mission between me, Damien, and Eric. You are not needed or wanted right now. Brandon, take Amara out, please."

"But—" she sputtered, wide-eyed.

"Mara. Go. Now," I commanded, growling with irritation. She was a problem I didn't have time for at the moment. "This doesn't concern you. We'll talk soon."

Her face softened, and she gave me a nod before leaving the room with Brandon.

"What's going on," I demanded the moment they were gone.

"Don't freak out, OK," Eric started.

"How the hell do you expect me to not freak out when you start a sentence with 'don't freak out'?"

"OK, sorry. Listen. Everly is in the hospital. She's in a coma," Eric tried again. Weakly, I got to my feet and went straight to my closet, my heart thudding in my ears. She was still hurting. I had to get to her. I had to fix her. Guilt washed over me for wanting her dead. It was so heavy I had to lean against the wall to steady myself. I rubbed at my chest and throat. Both still felt like they were on fire.

"Man, just rest. She'll be fine. You-you don't want to see her this way," Damien pleaded softly, his voice cracking.

"Why don't I?" I snapped, lifting my head to look at him. He shifted uncomfortably and looked away from me. "Just say it!"

"She's not breathing on her own. She hasn't been since she got there."

"I failed," I said, paling. "She was breathing when I passed out. I heard her! I felt her!"

"She was, man. But she had a lot of injuries. She had a brain injury. The doctors don't even know if she's going to wake up. If she'll even be the same again."

"Then I'll go heal her," I declared, trying to push off the wall.

"You aren't strong enough, man. Look at you! You're barely able to stand up! She's alive. I promise you that. Just please. Rest for today. Go tomorrow. I'll go stay with her. I'll report back every few hours. I swear it."

"If anything happens to her—" I said, my voice quaking, my stomach rolling with the thought.

"It won't. These are just precautions. They said her lungs were collapsed. She has some internal injuries and some broken bones. She's strong. She'll pull through. I'll make sure of it," Eric assured me.

"Stitch if you have to. Why didn't you stitch before it happened?"

"She ran out of the party with Dylan. We couldn't keep up with them. We got there too late," Damien continued, apologizing. "I'm so sorry, man."

I nodded. Shit happened. I couldn't blame them. They did all they could. If Eric wasn't near enough to her, he couldn't stop her from getting hurt. I knew he would have if he'd been able to keep up with her. I staggered back to my bed and sat down feeling woozy.

"Just rest. You need to relax. What you went through, well… it was pretty terrifying for lack of a better word," Damien added.

"Why?" I winced as I eased back against my pillows.

"You had a fever. A high one. Even Brandon couldn't help you while you were under. Adam offered to get Nevron Blackburn here to turn you into a vamp just in case you went south. I figured you'd be too pissed and would rather die than let that happen. So, we just sat here with you for the days you were under—"

"Wait. *Days?* How many days?" I held up a hand interrupting Eric, silently grateful that they hadn't gotten Nevron, the overlord's nephew to turn me. Nevron and I didn't see eye-to-eye at all. It was a mutual loathing. I'm sure he'd have loved to change me into the thing I hated.

"Nine," Damien coughed.

"*Nine? Nine days?*" I choked out.

"Speaking of which, you need to drink something. It was a mess dealing with you. Luckily, Amara did most of it. She'd have made a good Nattie nurse," Damien said reasonably. "Headmaster Brighton wanted to send you to the infirmary, but Eric, being next in command, thought keeping you here without everyone knowing you were hurt was a better option. Madame Ann has been in and out checking on you in the mornings."

"And the Order? Do they know?"

"We didn't tell them. We just said you were busy working and couldn't be bothered. I took care of all the missions and things," Eric explained. "But Sangrey isn't dumb. I think he knows something is going on. You might have to tell them what happened."

I nodded and drank down the glass of water he handed me before sinking back into my pillows, my guts still churning. As much as I didn't want them to take her, I knew I had to report it. *Maybe.* I had to make sure she pulled through first.

"Go to her," I said tiredly. "Check on her. I can feel her. Come to me immediately if she needs me."

"You know I will." Damien grasped my hand before disappearing.

"So," Eric said, walking forward and looking out my bedroom window. "It's true."

"Yeah," I answered softly.

"Are you afraid?"

"Only for her. I don't want her to become a victim. When I was talking to her that night, I could feel her terror at what was happening. She doesn't want to die. The fact that I was able to prevent it is astounding. I *felt* her dying. Everything around us felt distant." I shook my head. "It's hard to explain. It was like we were here... yet not. I've never encountered a soul like that before, but I felt hers." I grew quiet, my anger beginning to blanket me. "I'm such a jerk. I wanted to kill her before. When I saw her lying there..." my voice trailed off as I became choked up.

"I get it that you want to protect her now, but it nearly killed you." Eric turned and looked at me sadly.

"I can't really die either." I chuckled softly, pushing my tears back. I couldn't cry. I wouldn't. "I mean I can. But she can bring me back, too. At least that's how I think it works."

"And if it doesn't?" Eric's gaze leveled on me.

"I'll be fine. We're a circle. Infinity. Forever. Always," I answered, my voice barely above a whisper.

"So... what are you going to do now? No more thoughts on murdering the girl while she sleeps?"

"No. I'm going to keep her safe." I swallowed hard. "I need to get her here. I'm going to the Order to let them know what she is—what we are. It's the only way to get the ball rolling on getting her here at Dementon. You know she'll be safer here than anywhere else."

Eric nodded without saying anything.

"I'm worried sick about her. She's mine, you know?" I cleared my throat and stared guiltily at him. "I feel for her. And I hate that I do. I don't want to. But it's there, tearing me apart. How can you hate someone you care so much for?" Admitting it out loud caused me to close my eyes in an effort to hold back the dam of tears threatening to erupt. When I'd composed myself enough, I opened my eyes. The skin on my wrist prickled. Without looking at it, I turned my focus back to Eric.

"You're in some shit, man." Eric came and sat on the chair beside my bed, his blue eyes focused on me. "Do you even know what you want?"

"Not really," I sighed helplessly. "I just know that I won't kill her. And I know that I don't want to drag her into this. But I know that I can never be with her, no matter how much my soul begs for me to be." Swallowing hard, I fist my sheet in my hands. I wished I could get over everything, and I wished it wasn't so dangerous for us to be together. "I know I should let her go. I know that I don't want to tell the Order about our truth, and yet I know it's the only way to get her here and get her the help she needs. Those are the things I know," my voice became soft as the words tumbled out.

"Do you want to be with her?" Eric asked gently.

"No," I said fiercely. "Not like *this*. I want her to have a choice in it. I'll never force her. I'll never pursue her in that way. I can't. She can *never* know me."

"You're playing with fire," Eric murmured. "Trying to bring her here. That's like presenting a side of beef to a starving werewolf. How will you stay away? Especially once the Order knows? She's going to find out about you."

"I don't know," I said painfully. He was right. Maybe telling the Order wasn't such a good idea. They'd want her in Conexus. I didn't want this life for her. If I could keep her out of Conexus, then she'd never know me. Maybe I could just keep up the charade that she was just a normal Special, if there was such a thing. "Honestly, I just want this to go away. I want her to be able to live without being afraid. If she can learn to do that here, then this is where she needs to be. My feelings be damned."

"Are you going to talk to Amara about all of this? She isn't going to take it very well if she finds out Everly's the mancer and you're the reever. You know that, right?" Eric grew quiet again, as did I. He was right. Amara was going to lose her shit. "What are you going to do?"

"I'm going to go see Everly as soon as I can," I answered tightly.

"And somewhere in all that, I'm going to break it off with Amara. We haven't been good in a long time. I've always felt I needed to be somewhere else. And now I know why and where. That doesn't change anything though. It'll just mean at least Amara won't be hurt through it all."

"How do you even know what you feel for Everly is real? That it's just not part of the Wards?"

"My heart reacts to her." I chuckled softly, a smile tipping my lips as I imagined her. "Whenever I think about her, it beats madly in my chest. I didn't realize how much she meant until I saw her lying there in her own blood. But... I still hate her." The words were thick in my mouth and hard to utter, a complete contradiction to whatever these feelings in my heart were. I was a confused ball of anger. "I care. If that makes any sense. She has to prove me wrong. She deserves that chance."

Eric's lip curved up into a knowing smirk, and he nodded.

"I get you, man. We'll get her here. And we'll keep her safe. Then she'll prove to you that she's worth it. That girl is a fighter. I knew it the moment I saw her."

"I just don't want this for her," I sighed. "For either of us. And I sure as hell don't want her to feel obligated to *want* me if she ever finds out. I don't want her to know what she is, not in the same manner as we do. She can come here, join the psychic faction, and just learn to control her abilities. She doesn't need to know more than that. There are plenty of psychics here who have a weak ability to commune with the dead."

"Not like her though. She's going to stick out. You know she will."

"Every great Special sticks out a little bit more than the rest," I reminded him. "It's what gets them into Conexus."

Eric nodded thoughtfully.

"You think that's a good idea, though?" Eric frowned. "Keeping that from her? What she is?"

"I do," I nodded. "At least for now. And I want to keep her out of Conexus. The Order is going to want her to join. But I do *not* want this life for her."

"You act like our lives are so bad," Eric chuckled.

"*We* didn't get a choice," I replied. "I want Everly to have a choice."

"The one you didn't give Amara?" Eric ventured delicately.

"Yeah," I answered sourly. "But I wasn't *with* Amara when she joined us. I choose our members. Everly will never be one. I couldn't handle being near her without wanting her."

# CHAPTER 17

*I* awoke with a start and a heaviness in my chest, my wrist burning. I rubbed my fingers over the symbol that had finally revealed itself fully. The perfect oval, like a zero, had been on the tender skin of my wrist since birth. Mom used to kiss it, said it made me special, unique. Over time little lines here and there had popped up near it. I'd always wondered if it was some secret message waiting to be decoded. Now it was complete. Two joined zeros, a figure eight. Infinity. The lines were fully connected when I came to after saving Everly.

The weight in my chest pressed harder. It was mid-afternoon the following day, and I'd spent most of the previous night and today trying to recover.

"Everly," I whispered, pushing the covers off me. There was a knock on my door. "Enter."

Damien pushed the door open with Eric behind him.

"It's her," I said, climbing uneasily to my feet.

"She's awake," Damien answered. "And she's breathing on her own."

"I'm going to her," I said immediately. My friends looked at one another, a silent conversation spoken between them.

"We'll go with you," Eric finally said, looking over to me. I nodded, and they left me to dress. Quickly, I put on a clean black uniform and my cloak, then studied myself in the mirror. I'd managed a shower late the night before. This was the first day of our new life. I touched the red infinity symbol marking the underside of my wrist. My heart skipped in my chest, worry setting in. *What if she hated me?* That was a hell of a way to spend an eternity. I didn't know Everly well. I just knew the scared girl from when we were kids. I didn't know her now. I just knew she didn't want to die. And she was beautiful.

I drew in a deep breath, my aquamarine eyes near-glowing as I focused on trying to heal myself. Surprisingly, warmth spread through me immediately as my body strengthened. I'd struggled with getting it to work since I'd woken up. This was a good sign!

Feeling a million times better, I pushed my silver hair back from my face and tied it into a small ponytail at the back of my head. Satisfied with how I looked, I left the bathroom and went downstairs to find Damien and Eric waiting for me. And everyone else in our chapter.

A round of applause greeted me. Eric told me no one knew what had happened to me. Only that I'd been on a secret mission and had been hurt.

"Thank you," I murmured, my eyes finding Amara's. She came to me and wrapped her arms around me tightly. I didn't hug her or even kiss her back when she pressed her mouth to mine.

"We have cake!" Adam proclaimed, gesturing to a large chocolate cake on the coffee table in the center of the room.

"Sorry, Shadow. We tried to tell them you didn't want any of this." Damien shrugged helplessly. I let out a sigh and forced a tight smile. Everything in me only wanted to check on my girl. My Everly.

"I appreciate everything you've all done," I said, as everyone hushed. Amara wrapped her arms around my waist and rested her head against my shoulder as I spoke. I glanced down at her feeling frustrated. "However, I'm unable to join you at this time. Duty calls."

There was a general moan of letdown.

"Save him a piece of cake," Eric called out.

"Screw it. I'm eating." Jared shrugged, going to the cake. Sloane grinned and handed him the knife, and I was soon forgotten about. It wasn't unusual for me to skip out on events.

"Are you *kidding* me?" Amara hissed. "You're leaving? *Again*? You've only just healed!"

"I have a responsibility," I said firmly.

"You promised we'd spend time together. Where are you off to this time? And why can't I go?"

"You *know* where I'm going. Don't act like you don't," I snapped at her.

"To her? The Nattie?"

"She isn't a Nattie," I replied, unwinding her arms from around my waist. "She's a Special, and she'll be coming to Dementon as soon as the Order gives their approval. I'm meeting with them tomorrow over the matter."

"I hope she does come here," Amara snarled, her eyes flashing dangerously. "Because I want to meet this girl. I want her to know who she's messing with—"

"I'm not listening to this. I'm leaving. But you and I," I whispered through my clenched teeth and narrowed my eyes at her, we'll talk later."

"You're damn right we will!"

She stomped away from me with a roll of her eyes. I let out a frustrated sigh, more at myself than anything. I should've ended things with her a long time ago.

"Forget it, man." Damien patted me on the shoulder. "You're done there anyway, right?"

"Yeah," I muttered, turning to leave. He and Eric fell in step behind me as we went out to the street.

"She's at Mercy," Eric said, indicating the hospital. I gave a tight nod as I turned to meld, Eric and Damien following suit. We quickly whisked through the darkness, and before I knew it, I was standing outside the hospital.

"It's going to be hard to go in there without her seeing you. It's easy to stay hidden from the Natties. Harder when it's another

Special, *especially* one like her. There are very few shadows in there to blend in with," Damien said, gazing up at the brick monstrosity in front of us.

"I'll figure it out," I murmured, knowing I could create what I needed to.

"Don't heal her." Eric turned to face me. "No matter what. If you do, things will look suspicious. You have to let this happen, OK?"

"Like hell—"

"Listen, man! If you heal her, how can it be explained to the Natties? It'll only cause her more problems. You're going to have to sit this one out. OK?"

I nodded. He was right. And I hated it.

"And don't kill her," Eric added as an afterthought. I snorted at him, shaking my head. That was the last thing I planned on doing.

"We'll come with you. Just in case," Damien added. I rolled my eyes at him but agreed. I knew I'd need them to stop me from healing her completely if it came down to it. We traveled upstairs, once again using any shadows we could. It was like skipping through puddles as we hopped from one shadow to the next, something that was proving difficult inside of the hospital. I created what I could, which helped.

Once I made it to her room, I was grateful to find her sleeping with no visitors.

"We'll keep watch," Damien grunted at the door. I gave him a curt nod and approached her bed.

As I stared down at her, I drew in a sharp breath. Her face was badly bruised. The purple and red patches ignited anger deep within me. *Dylan.* I'd make him pay for this. Her arm was wrapped and so was her leg. A bandage wound around her head, and she was paler than usual, which made her eyes really stand out in their black and blue state. Even her plump pink lips were cracked. My heart squeezed.

"Sweetheart," I murmured, reaching out to touch her face gently. I glanced in the direction of my friends and was grateful they weren't looking at me. I quickly sent a bit of energy out to her, healing some of the nasty bruises to a dull yellow color. I even gave the gash I knew was hiding beneath the bandage on her head a quick nudge in healing, so it wouldn't scar so badly.

"Ever, I'm so sorry this is happening to you. I'll take care of you from now on. I promise I will. I'll do what I have to do to keep you safe. It's going to be a rough road, Everly, but I swear to you it's worth it. Just hang on for me, OK?" I leaned in and planted a gentle kiss on her cheek.

"Mm," she murmured, her hand moving. It found mine as she slept, and she gave it a tiny squeeze. "Shadow."

My heart lurched in my chest. I didn't realize how involved I really was until that moment. I only wanted to help her. But she'd caught me. And she had me. And I didn't even want her to let me go despite knowing in my heart that she deserved so much more than the life I could offer her. I knew I couldn't keep her. It wasn't fair to her. It would only cause her more pain. Instead, I vowed to just protect her. To keep her safe from all I could. I'd never tell her who I was. Which meant I couldn't get close to her any longer because if I did, I wouldn't be able to control myself from claiming her for good and sealing our destiny.

All we could ever be was me staring at her from across a crowded room, wishing I wasn't me.

.

# CHAPTER 18

"**Y**ou're more sullen than usual," Eric commented as we left the hospital. I'd kissed her tenderly on her forehead before leaving her there. I had to let things play out. I knew I did.

"I have to let her go," I replied, my voice stronger than I expected it to be.

"What?" Damien asked. I didn't answer him until we were back on Dementon grounds.

"Because. She deserves more than what I can give her. She deserves a choice. I *won't* take it from her."

The guys were quiet as we walked to our house on the edge of campus.

"And Amara?" Eric ventured.

"Over. I can't give her what she wants either. Not when I love someone else."

"Wait. You really *love* Everly?" Eric asked. Damien gave a low whistle.

"Yeah," I answered, accepting it. It was the only explanation I had for my feelings for her. The moment she was out of my sight, I was left breathless, a burning desire to breathe her in, my chest aching for her. She was in my mind constantly. I had endless thoughts about what it would be like to just hold her in my arms for eternity. If that wasn't love, I didn't know what was.

"Shadow, man, you can't live your life avoiding the one person you're *meant* to be with—" Eric started.

"I have to. I'll protect her, but I can't get involved with her. Us together is too dangerous. Can you imagine what would happen if anyone found out what we were? Do you know what could happen to all of us? Even you guys? If the Cipher got her, she could create an army so vast, drawing all the souls to her to raise up from the Veil. They'd take down the Order. They'd take over both the Nattie and Special world. She needs to be kept safe and as unknown as possible. I won't let anyone be a pawn in this war. No way. It's my job to protect you guys. I won't fail."

"I think you need to reconsider—" Eric argued.

"This is my reconsideration," I snapped. "It's done. Before it even started. I'm going to stay away from her. We'll pop in less on her. I think she's hidden enough that she won't have issues. If we keep going to her, it could draw attention to her. Nothing's bothered her since I sent the wraith back to the void."

"You're the boss," Damien muttered. "So... Does that mean I can introduce myself to her?" I knew he was joking with me, but it upset me just the same. The idea of anyone with their hands on her made my stomach twist into uncomfortable knots. I shot him a nasty look. "Damn, boss. Just askin'!"

When we made it into the house a few members of Conexus were still in the commons, lounging around.

"You're back!" Sloane exclaimed, her dark eyes meeting mine. She narrowed them at me for a moment before getting to her feet and stopping in front of me. "You're upset. Talk to me. It's girl troubles. I can tell."

"Uh..." I looked between Eric and Damien who only grinned and shrugged. Sloane had a way of being able to detect all of our problems.

"Seriously. Let's talk. I need to vent about something anyway, too." Without waiting for me to answer, she tugged me by my hand and led me to my office where she closed the door behind us. "Spill. Now."

"There's nothing to spill," I muttered, flopping down in my chair and rubbing my eyes.

"Bullshit," Sloane raised her dark eyebrows at me. "Spill it or I'll quit Conexus."

"You can't quit Conexus! This is a lifelong bid. You know that—"

"Doesn't matter. I'll still quit—or turn you into a toaster. We'll see if your shifter prince ass can get out of that. Your choice."

"You're a pain in the ass, Monroe," I grumbled, but grinned. A girl's perspective might actually help me.

"Come on." She flopped down on the couch against my wall. I got out of my chair and went and sat beside her nervously, which was unheard of for me. I was *never* nervous. "Talk to me. Nothing said here will leave this room. I swear it."

"Swear?" I raised an eyebrow at her.

"I'll blood oath it if I have to," she countered, pulling out her knife.

"I trust you," I mused. She pocketed her knife and stared at me.

"Speak. I know you have a lot going on in that gorgeous head of yours. You've been acting strange for weeks now."

"I'm in love," I said softly. She let out a sputtering cough before shaking it off quickly.

"Wait. What?"

"I'm in love," I repeated, my heart fluttering as I thought of my sweet Everly.

"You just realized you're in love with Amara?" She crinkled her brows. "I don't understand how this is a problem—"

"It's not Amara." Sighing, I rubbed my eyes, even more frustrated. I sounded like the worst person ever. I was in love with someone, and it wasn't my girlfriend. And I'd wanted to kill the girl I was in love with, and somehow still hated her. I was a mess. *Great.*

"Oh, wow." Sloane shifted in her seat. "It's me, isn't it?"

"You're such a shit," I chuckled at her trying to help me loosen up. She grinned back at me, her dark eyes shining.

"So, who really is the lucky girl?" She nudged me. "How did you meet her?"

"Her name is Everly," I answered. "I've known her since we were just kids." I decided I had to tell her the whole story, so I did. She listened, frowning more than smiling. Once I finished she let out a sigh.

"She doesn't even know who you are. This is a *freaking* tragic romance. Why don't you just tell her you love her? Why don't you just let yourself feel for once? And stop thinking you hate her. You don't *hate* her. You hate the situation. You hate your mom being gone. You hate mustard. But Everly? Nope. You love that girl."

"I can't. It's too dangerous for her. I want to keep her safe. I owe her that."

"Listen to me. She's going to love you, you know that, right? Just because you guys have a shitty sounding destiny together, doesn't mean anything. You have the control. You can make it as beautiful or as tragic as you want. I trust that you know your heart better than anyone. I know you'll do what you feel is right by her, even if it's staying away. I can't tell you what to do there except let the seed grow. Don't try to halt it. That's how things get twisted and ugly. Let nature take its course. I can tell you this though, you're a good guy. You need to tell Amara that it's over between you two. I'm not a big fan of hers, and you two never made sense to me."

"Really?" I asked. Everyone else seemed to think we made sense together.

"Really. You're a hard ass, yes. But she doesn't challenge you. I think this girl will. I think you need her in your life. You'll be able to grow with her. With Amara, you'll only find yourself arguing and doing the same thing over and over. You two fight, kiss, make up and then do it all over again, but are you happy doing that? I mean, come on."

"I'm not happy. You're right."

"Even if you decide to keep your distance from this Everly girl, at least you won't be the jerk who dragged out a dying, failing sham of a relationship. End it. Seriously. If you have any doubts, you need to put the brakes on and g.t.f.o. Because if you don't, and you find yourself able to pursue Everly, Amara will be hurt. Everly will be hurt by it. And so will you. Save some heartache and cut the damn cord."

"When did you get so smart, Monroe?" I mused.

"Isn't that why you forced me into Conexus?" she asked innocently. I snorted at her and shook my head.

"I pulled you in because you're one of the best casters I've ever seen," I answered honestly.

"Yeah, well, that's kinda what I wanted to talk to you about. I, uh, I want to talk to my friends again. I'm lonely here. I don't fit in," she didn't meet my eyes as she said the words.

"I know you're lonely," I said softly. "I'm sorry, for what it's worth. You know the dangers of associating with people outside of Conexus. They become targets in the event of something bad. I don't want that for anyone. It's another reason why I'm staying away from Everly. Why I won't talk to her. It's for her safety. I know you miss your friends, Sloane. And I'm sorry that it's this way. But no. You can't talk to them. I'm not doing it to be a jerk. I'm doing it to protect you and them. You understand that, right?"

"I guess," she mumbled, her dark curls falling over her shoulder. "Rules and all that. Policies. Procedures. Crap."

"Have you tried getting along with Amara? Or Chloe and Amanda?"

"Amara is just too mean for me." Sloane sighed. "And Chloe and Amanda are OK, but they're best friends. I just want to have some fun. I'm trapped here, though."

"Damien is fun," I pointed out. Her lips turned up.

"He is," she said, still grinning. "I guess I can torment him until he comes to you to make me go away."

"See? Now you've got a plan."

We sat in silence for a moment before she got to her feet.

"Talk to Amara. Do it for the both of you. And when you're done, go to Everly and look at her and see how you feel then. And please, don't think about killing Everly again."

"I won't," I murmured. She gave me a sad smile as she left the room.

She was right. I had to end things with Amara.

# CHAPTER 19

"Hey," Amara greeted me at her bedroom door. She opened it, and I stepped inside.

"Hey," I replied following her to her bed. We sat down next to each other on it, and she stared at me expectedly. "We need to talk."

"OK," she answered, her voice shaking. She reached for my hand, but I pulled away and put a safe amount of space between us.

"I've been doing some thinking." I cleared my throat. "And I think it's time you and I call it quits."

"What?" her voice shook harder, tears springing to her eyes.

"I'm not in a good place right now, Mara. Being with you is doing you an injustice. You deserve to be with someone who loves you as much as you love them. I am not that guy."

"Wow," she breathed out, clearing her throat as a tear slipped out of her eye. "Are we taking a break? Or is this really over, over?"

"It's really over," I said gently. She grew quiet and clasped her trembling hands.

"Is it because of this Everly? Are you in love with her?"

"Amara, it's because of me. I'm a mess in my head. And I don't want to bring Everly into this—" I waved my hand, gesturing between the two of us.

"But it's true, isn't it?"

"A few weeks ago I stood in her bedroom plotting her murder," I said softly. "Now, after all we've been through with each other, I feel for her, yes. But I never acted on it in any way other than keeping her safe. We've spoken twice in fourteen years. She doesn't even know who I am. And *nothing* will ever happen between me and her. So please, don't run with the idea that I'm leaving you for her because I'm not. I'm doing this because it's time. I'm not happy. You're not happy. It's turned into just sex and fights with us. I know you want more than that. And I can't give it to you. I know that if we keep this up, our parents will force us into marriage. I really don't want that. I want to marry when I'm ready for it. I want to genuinely marry for love."

"And you've never loved me," her voice was laced with pain and heartache.

"Mara, don't do this," I pleaded gently.

"I need to hear you say it."

"*Why?*" I asked, exasperated. "What will it change?"

"I need to know," her voice wavered as she looked at me with glassy eyes, some of the tears already slipping silently down her cheeks.

"I care about you," I said softly, looking down at my hands. "But no, I'm not in love with you."

"I need you to leave," she sniffled, balling her hands into fists. "Now."

I rose from my seat.

"Amara, I'm really sorry. Truly. I-I never meant to hurt you—"

"Please. Just go." She let out a soft cry. I backed away from her, watching as her body shook. There wasn't anything I could do about that though. Instead, I slipped out the door, closing it softly behind me, feeling like the worst person in the world.

# CHAPTER 20

The weeks passed by painfully. My heart was in disarray at being away from Everly, but the thought of being near her gave me moments of insanity. I'd ordered Eric and Damien to stop going to her daily. Instead, they checked in on her once a week, two tops. I'd gone to the Order and asked for her to be brought to Dementon. I didn't mention anything about her being the Mancer. I didn't want to confirm it for them and put her in even more danger. Instead, I opted to say I felt she'd benefit greatly from our school. The Order agreed to take it to a vote at the next meeting before passing it down to the school board to deal with.

Over the passing weeks, I barely ate or slept. I did missions, tore down haunts, and took out the Cipher as assigned, hauling them kicking and screaming to Xanan to be dealt with.

"You realize you're fighting for the wrong side, don't you?" a vamp Cipher snarled at me on my most recent encounter with our opposition. "The Order are the ones you *should* be fighting! You're just a blind fool! We *know* the Mancer has been born! We'll find her!"

I silenced him with a stake through the heart, not an ounce of remorse tainting me.

"That was interesting," Damien commented, wiping his blade on an old curtain in the Cipher nest we'd just decimated.

"He was spouting lies. It's all they're good for," I growled, wiping at my brow. I leaned against the wall, suddenly feeling ill.

"Everly," I said her name softly.

"Is she OK?" Eric asked, hearing me.

"She's scared. Terrified." I stared fearfully at Eric and Damien.

"I'll go," Eric stated firmly. "I'll report back as soon as I know anything."

He didn't wait for me to say anything. He simply melded into the shadows and disappeared.

"We cleared out everything in this place," Adam proclaimed, coming into the room, Sloane, Brandon, Amanda, Chloe, and Amara behind him. Amara and I had barely spoken to one another since our breakup.

Damien grinned as they straggled in before looking over to Sloane, his eyes lighting up. "Hey, babe. You ever kill a caster?"

She rolled her eyes at him. "Just the carrion who get tainted by the rest of the messed-up factions. You never see a real caster out there being a total screw up."

"Pity," he sighed, his eyes moving over to Amara.

"Don't start with me, Wick," Amara snarled before Damien could even open his mouth.

"You're moodier than usual now that Shadow has moved on. Does that translate to rougher sex with weres?" Damien asked innocently.

"I'm going to kick your ass," Amara growled at him, taking a dangerous step toward him.

"Sounds like foreplay." He winked at her.

"Amara, come on," Brandon sighed. "He's just trying to irritate you. Just chill. I'm hungry and don't want to deal with this shit tonight."

I caught Amara's eye. She cast me an angry glare before stomping out of the room in her tight, black hunting outfit.

"Dude, if you're hard up, you should tap that shit now. I bet some good old hate sex will soothe both your wounds," Damien advised me.

"Shut up," I snarled, not in the mood for his teasing. I was feeling sicker by the minute.

"Wick, why are you always such an ass?" Chloe demanded.

"Babe, you wound me." Damien feigned grabbing at his broken heart. "I'm a sweetheart. Right, Sloane?"

"Yeah, if that means you're an egotistical dumbass," Sloane remarked, causing both Chloe and Amanda to laugh loudly.

"Love you too, babe." Damien winked at Sloane who grinned at him. I wondered when they'd stop fighting and actually get together since they so clearly liked one another.

"You don't look so good, Gen," Brandon observed. "Did a vamp bite you or something?"

"No." I shook my head, my hair falling forward into my eyes. "I just need to get home. We're done for tonight."

"Woo!" Adam whooped, grinning. We melded and made our way back to our common room. Once there, I went straight to my room and showered before finding my bed. I fell into a fitful sleep with Everly on my mind.

# CHAPTER 21

"*H*ey," Eric's urgent voice roused me from my sleep. I sat up and stared at him blearily.

"Is she OK?"

"Yeah, if by OK you mean she's seeing the freaking dead at every turn and hearing voices."

"What?" I threw my blankets back and got out of bed. Dashing to my bathroom, I dressed in my all black hunting attire and came out, staring him down.

"Seems her abilities have been severely heightened since her accident. I've never felt the dead or creatures from the void so strongly before. They're surrounding her, man. They're under her bed, in her closet. She's being haunted. Bad. Their presence is so strong that even *I* can see them sometimes."

"What?" I repeated, my eyes widening. He nodded wordlessly.

"I know you wanted to keep your distance, but I think you need to go to her. Just check on her. See if there's anything you can do. She's so afraid. I almost showed myself to her just to calm her down."

"I'm going." I grabbed my blades and shoved them into their slots on my person before melding away. I went straight to her living room. I winced. Eric was right. The place was loaded with the dead.

"Stop! STOP IT!" Everly's pained voice shouted out desperately from her kitchen, the sound of silverware clattering to the floor. "Stop! Please!"

"Ever!" I heard her mom's voice.

"Make them stop, *Mamá*. Please!" Everly begged, sobbing.

"Make what stop, baby?" her mom's scared voice called out.

"The voices. The-the people. . . the dead people. Make them go away!"

"Ever?" her friend Nina's voice came out frightened.

I stopped listening after that because a wraith slithered from beneath her couch, its hollow sockets focused on Everly's voice in the other room not even noticing me. I raced forward and rammed my blade through its torso. There was a grotesque sucking noise as it sizzled and disappeared.

I burst into the kitchen, not caring if she saw me. Her eyes immediately locked on mine as her friend tried to calm her down. My heart broke in that instant for her all over again. She was so frail as she sat there, her eyes glassy with unshed tears and filled with her unspoken fears.

"No, it's not," she whispered. I took a step toward her, this overwhelming urge to make everything go away washing over me. I concentrated on it so hard all the sounds around us faded away, leaving us in silence. It had worked. I'd blocked them.

She let out a breath as she gazed at me.

"Everything will never be OK again."

She had no idea how right she was.

# CHAPTER 22

*I* disappeared after that. I went immediately to Headmaster Brighton's office and barged in like I owned the place.

"I was just going to summon you," Brighton said as I came into the room.

"Yeah, then maybe we're on the same page here. Everly Torres. Are you familiar with the name?"

"Quite." He nodded. "She's been on my radar for a few years now thanks to the Order's desire for me to watch her."

"Why?" I demanded.

"Well, the Order asks that I keep tabs on potential Specials, especially those of the psychic variety. She never displayed any abilities past the age of twelve. So, I assumed she was just like other sensitive Nattie children. Of course, with this new dilemma I can see that we're in a bit deep with her. In fact, I was just summoned by one of my connections to go to her. I'll be meeting with her shortly."

"You're meeting with her?" I wasn't sure why that bothered me so much. Maybe because I knew Brighton would report his findings to the Order, and I didn't want them to know so much about it. On the other hand, I knew better than anyone that Brighton knew his shit and would see to it that she was taken care of.

"I am." He stopped putting papers into his briefcase and looked at me. "Is there anything I should know about?"

"She's in trouble. You know that which I speak of?"

"Of course. Is it true then? Is she the Mancer?"

"No," I snapped, lying. I couldn't have him knowing that bit of information. "But she is an untrained Special who's being haunted. She needs to make it here to Dementon. Do whatever you need to do to make that happen. Got it?"

"On whose orders?" Headmaster Brighton sighed. "You know I can't intervene—"

"My orders," I growled. "I'll take care of the Order."

"I don't doubt you will." He chuckled and looked at me thoughtfully. "I'll be honest with you, I've thought for a long time that she needed to be evaluated and brought here. Now I can confirm it. I'll make sure she makes it here. You just need to be patient. This could be quite beneficial."

"I know it could be."

We regarded one another silently for a moment. I knew that he knew I was full of shit. He knew what she was just as well as I did. "Will she be a Conexus recruit?" he asked the question easily.

"Never," I answered softly, my guts churning as the thought of my beautiful girl engaged in deadly battle erupted into my mind.

"Ah, I see." He smiled kindly at me. "I know you care for the girl. You've been in and out of here for weeks dealing with it. So have Mr. Craft and Mr. Wick. I read the reports." He winked at me. "I know you all think I don't, but I do. Allow me to get to this, then, eh? You must understand that this could take some time. It's hard to convince a parent to let their child come to a place like this when they aren't familiar with our world, which is why we do things the way we do. Everly taking a turn like this might be just what we need to make it happen. This could be a very good thing indeed."

"I don't care. Just see to it that she's helped."

"You know I will." He nodded solemnly at me as he rose to his feet. He grabbed his jacket from the closet, looking every bit the part of a psychiatrist that he moonlighted as in the Nattie world. He was how we got a lot of our students there. He kept a watch over the troubled ones who had no idea what or who they were. Many of them made their way to his facility where he tested them and brought them to Dementon where they were able to understand their abilities. Brighton was a Fae who specialized in reading emotions. And he could sense thoughts, almost like a telepath.

"Please let me know how she's doing," I said as we walked out of his office.

"You know how patient doctor confidentiality works," he sighed, stopping on the steps outside the building.

"She's important to me," I answered fiercely, the truth of the words coursing painfully through me.

"I know she is," he murmured as he looked up at me. "I'll do what I can, General." I watched as he climbed into one of our black SUVs and drove toward the Dementon gates. When he was gone, I went back to the Conexus house wondering if Everly was doing OK.

"How'd it go?" Eric asked, coming to me as I stood in the kitchen watching Damien make a sandwich.

"Headmaster Brighton is intercepting her as we speak. She'll be in good hands. He'll be able to keep track of her and how bad things get. Hopefully, he'll be able to get her here eventually."

"Good," Eric nodded. "What about us? Are we going back on mission?"

"I think so. Just to check in on her. This is going to be rough for her. When I was in her house, I felt what you said. It was thick in there. They were *everywhere*."

"Did you magic palm any of them?" Damien asked, taking a large bite of his turkey sub.

"No, but I did take out a wraith. It's weird," I said thoughtfully. "I wanted them gone, and I focused on it. And just like that, they were."

"Maybe you're her shield. I mean, if you protect her, then it only makes sense," Eric put in.

"True," I murmured. I was just about to say more to them about it when Amara and Sloane came into the kitchen.

"Hey," I greeted them awkwardly. Sloane beamed at me, but Amara only scowled at me.

"That time of the month?" Damien asked mildly, a twinkle in his eye as he looked at Amara.

"I don't shift until later," she growled at him which only made him grin wider. The tension was too thick. I cleared my throat and tried to make nice.

"How are you doing, Mara?" I asked.

"Shouldn't you be creeping around the shadows somewhere in some poor girl's bedroom?" she sneered nastily at me. Everyone grew quiet.

"You're right. I have to go." I pushed off the counter not wanting to make a scene. "I hope you start feeling better, Mara. See you guys." I didn't wait for an answer. I made my way up to my room and flopped down in bed with no intention of going near Everly.

# CHAPTER 23

The following weeks passed by slowly. Painstakingly slow. I made sure we all kept our distance from Everly. As much as it tore me up, I knew it was important because these things needed to happen if we were going to get her to Dementon under the guise of her needing the school's help. I just hoped it didn't push her too close to the edge.

Eric, Damien, Brandon, and I walked through the Dementon campus in a tight-knit mass of black uniforms, cloaks, and stern faces. We all were armed, as was our typical style. I had to do an inspection after we got out of classes to make sure the walls were secure. The students left on the grounds rushed away from us, afraid to be nearby anything that had to do with our group. I was used to it. I liked it that way. We were the law of our land, and it was important that people remembered that.

We stopped at the limits, the place where our world met the Nattie world. Eric reached out and touched the large brick wall, nodding his approval at me. It was warded. Sloane and Jared had done a great job. The wards deterred the Natties and kept anything rogue out.

We proceeded to check the entire grounds before going to sit at our usual table. I was listening to Damien rag on Eric when a shadow was cast over me.

"Do you think life would be easier here for the students if you Conexus members didn't walk around on the grounds like you ruled the world?" a deep familiar voice cut through my thoughts on how to get more protection for the school before Everly got there.

"Nevron, what an unpleasant surprise." Eric didn't miss a beat as he looked to the large, blond haired vampire with the black eyes who sneered down at us. Nevron liked to test his limits by not drinking blood. Vampire eyes turned black right before they would blood lust. I vowed the moment his eyes shifted from black to red, I'd stake him myself.

"Oh, and look. He brought a friend." Damien grinned as Marcus Ambrose, an amber-eyed warlock with hair as black as night joined Nevron.

"Aren't you cute, Wick. Tell me, what's it like being the general's lap dog?" Marcus smirked.

"I'm no lap dog," Damien growled, getting to his feet.

"Said the mutt," Nevron retorted, as Damien began to shake, ready to shift.

"Damien," I warned, rising to my feet. Damien let out an angry hiss but calmed himself. "Nevron Blackburn and Marcus Ambrose don't pay a visit to anyone unless they want something. So, tell me..." I glared at them. "What do you want?"

"Are you always this much fun?" Nevron's red lips curved up into a broad smile.

"Always. Now get to the point," I replied evenly. I took a step toward them and noted how anyone left in the square had backed away. They knew I had a short temper and meant business. Nevron and Marcus were the campus cool guys. I didn't trust them as far as I could throw them, and most of that had to do with the fact that Nevron was related to Aviram. And Marcus's family had a history of being deeply involved with the Cipher. It only made sense that the two were best friends. However, I'd never found any dirt on either of them to warrant an interrogation or a trip to Xanan. They kept their noses clean, but they held a lot of power. After the Conexus on campus, they were the next feared. I didn't care for either of them. Even if Nevron hadn't been a vamp, I would've hated the guy.

"Rumor has it that there have been a lot of wraiths and carrion in the area. And even talk of lost ones. I figured I'd go right to the source of the law around here and find out if any of it were true." Nevron didn't waste time getting to his point.

"I'd think that *you* would already know the answer to that," I answered dangerously, trying to goad them into admitting anything they might know about the recent influx of dark creatures and dead.

"Why would you think that, General?" Nevron cocked his head at me, that irritating smirk on his lips.

"The first guess is free," I answered. Nevron and Marcus grinned knowingly at one another, the act making me want to pummel them right then and there. My guys must have sensed that because they flanked me.

"Do you have any idea how stupid you sound accusing *us* of being part of something you deem so evil? I'm appalled." Marcus shook his head sadly at us.

"You *are* a part of it," Damien snarled. "You just need to screw up, so we can prove it. And then it's bye-bye bitches."

Marcus let out a low growl, as a flame erupted in each hand and his amber eyes flashed dangerously. We couldn't have a showdown right in the middle of the school grounds. Nevron must have sensed that, or maybe he was smart enough to count. Since there were four of us and only two of them, an ass-whooping was imminent. He reached out and pushed Marcus's hands down. The flames flickered and went out.

Had the two of them not had such a history about them, they'd have made excellent members in Conexus. Both were two of the strongest creatures I'd ever seen. I just couldn't bring myself to induct them. They had a warning sign written all over them. And I refused to let a vamp into our ranks. I didn't care how good that vamp was.

"We aren't looking for trouble, General," Nevron said, his voice serious. "I was simply curious. We attend classes here. It'd be a shame if students stepped outside the limits and something terrible happened to them."

"Nothing terrible will happen. We're patrolling the area as always," I replied back.

"Fair enough." He nodded. As he started to turn away, he apparently had a thought because a tiny smirk appeared on his lips again. "Oh, I heard word that there may be a mancer running around these parts. Have you guys heard anything like that?"

"There is *no* mancer," my voice was low. "If there was, I'd be aware of it."

"Of course you would." Nevron's black eyes held a glint of knowing in them.

"Your eyes are black, Nev. I think you should go eat. I heard vamps get dumber when they haven't drunk in a few hours," Damien broke in.

"Cute, Wick. But just so you know, I *like* being hungry. It makes my days so much more exciting when I don't know if I'll lash out and chew through the student body here."

He didn't wait for a reply. He turned and walked away from us, Marcus at his side.

"I hate that guy," Brandon muttered. He'd been silent the entire time. I liked that about him. He was more of an action guy, not a talker.

"You're not the only one," I answered, my eyes still focused on their retreating backs. I wanted to get something on them so bad but had always come up empty-handed. I'd pretty much come to the conclusion they were probably legitimately not involved in the Cipher and just had to live up to the reputation that preceded them. *But where had they heard about a mancer?* I frowned deeply. Something had to be up with them. And I had no way to prove it other than by just simply keeping tabs on them like always.

I'd had enough excitement for the day. Classes were out, so we headed back to our house on the edge of campus, my guys talking the entire way of how to bait Nev and Marcus into admitting they were part of the Cipher.

*J* was sitting in my office later that evening, pouring over more research on the Wards, not finding anything I didn't already know, when there was a knock on my door.

"Come in," I said, pushing the papers into my drawer. The door cracked open and the sigil—my father—entered the room with Eric behind him.

"Father." I quickly got to my feet and bowed to him. "I didn't know you were coming."

"General," he acknowledged me. Eric cast me a raised eyebrow over my father's shoulder before closing the door, leaving me alone with him. "I hope I find you well."

"Yes." I nodded, moving back to my desk. "Have a seat. Would you like a drink?"

"I would, please," my father answered, his dark eyes following me as I moved to the small bar in my office. I reserved it for visitors like my father. Quickly, I poured both of us a tarish, a drink much like Nattie scotch, and handed him his while I sipped at mine.

"Forgive me, father. You *never* visit me. Is something wrong?" I asked, swallowing my drink.

"Isn't there always?" He threw back his drink, finishing it all. Jumping up, I fixed him another one, eyeing him suspiciously. My father wasn't the type of man to just show up to see me without reason.

"Then, to what do I owe the honor?"

"It's the girl. The one you came to the Order for." He took the glass from me, his dark gaze leveled on me.

"Oh?" I cleared my throat.

"Were you being honest when you spoke of going to her from a young age?" His eyes narrowed as he surveyed me.

"I was."

"Tell me, do you think me a fool?" he asked softly.

"I'm... sorry?"

"I know you're more than you let on, Son. Why do you think I've pushed you for so long and hard? You've *always* been special. You aren't like anyone else. Neither is the girl. Don't play me for a fool. Is it true?"

I studied him, a muscle thrumming along my jaw. It wasn't that I didn't trust my father. He was an honorable man. But he was the sigil, the king. And he wanted to keep his world just as safe as I did.

"How about this..." He placed his drink on my desk. "Tell me exactly what you can do. Leave nothing out."

"Sir—"

"I'm not asking as your sigil. I'm asking as your father." He stared evenly at me, waiting for me to speak. I sank down in my chair and sighed.

"It started when I was four. I was in bed. Mother had just read me a story, and I was just falling asleep. At first, I thought it was a dream, but then I realized it was real—the darkness, the voices, the claws on my skin. I saw a small girl, scared in her bedroom. I ran to the light. To her. When I came out of her closet, I was a shadow." I told him the story of how I visited her right up until she was twelve and then it had stopped abruptly.

"The last time I saw her was the night mother died. I went to her. That's why I left mother alone. I was *pulled* to Everly."

"I see," my father said softly, frowning at the news. "So, this *girl* is the reason your mother's gone?"

"That and a vampire decided to leech the life from her," I growled.

"And yet you continue to want to help the girl? Knowing that she's part of the reason your mother is dead?" He shook his head disgustedly. I didn't say anything. He was right. It was a war I'd been fighting with myself for weeks.

"And your abilities?" he asked after a moment of tense silence.

"I have many," I replied tightly. "I shift, like you. Sometimes I can sense things, almost like mother could, but not nearly as well. But there's more." I cleared my throat and sat forward, my hands clasped together as I stared evenly at him. "I can shift into a lock or a were. I can heal. I'm faster and stronger than any other member of Conexus."

"And?" my father prompted, eyeing me.

"I can bring Everly back." my voice was soft as I said the words. "She was in an accident a few weeks ago. She was dying. I sensed her and went. I let instinct guide me. I put my hands on her and took her death from her. I took her pain. And I lay unconscious here for nine days." I closed my eyes and sat quietly, waiting for whatever storm my father brought with him. *Was he going to command me to bring Everly there immediately? Make me induct her into Conexus?* I didn't want to tell him that mother told me this would happen with her.

"Are you marked?" his voice sounded odd. Opening my eyes, I stared at him. He seemed troubled, maybe even sad.

I hadn't even thought about the prophecy's reference to being marked. My mind tried and failed to recall the exact wording. Something about when the two combined they would go from zero to infinity. And they'd be marked accordingly. *Did Everly have a matching mark?* The thought made my heart jump. We might be marked for each other. Forever.

"I am," I whispered, rolling my sleeve up to show him the infinity symbol on my wrist.

"Do you love the girl?" he asked.

"I don't know what I feel anymore. I hated her. But I-I cared for her. Then it goes back to hate. I want to keep her safe, *that* much I know. I feel like she deserves a chance to prove herself. To prove that she's worth it all," I answered solemnly. "And... I feel lost without her. Incomplete. Empty. Sick. I'm in a state of constant worry. I can't focus or concentrate. She's on my mind every moment of every day, and yet I blame her for everything as much as I try not to. But keeping her safe outweighs it most days."

"It's the Wards." My father nodded slowly. "You're each other's other half, so it's only logical *that* force is drawing you to each another."

"It's not—"

"Son, it *is*. You do *not* love the girl," his voice was sharp and desperate as he got to his feet. "That hatred you feel? *That's* what's real! And it should be! If she wouldn't have pulled you to her, your mother would still be with us."

I didn't say anything. *What could I say?* It's not like I hadn't had the same thoughts over the course of the past few weeks. Hell, years even.

"She still needs help, Father," I replied softly. "We're capable of helping her. It's our job to help all, Natties and Specials alike."

My father's eyes swept over me a for a moment, his posture suggesting he had something on his mind.

"I don't deny the girl needs help, General," he finally spoke, his voice low. His eyes darted around my office before coming back to me. "I feel it's imperative that you're aware there's someone within the Order feeding our secrets to the Cipher."

"*What?*" I asked sharply, sitting forward in my seat.

My father nodded sadly. "I've suspected it for some time. I didn't say anything because I only have my suspicions to go on. But why are they after her? The dead? The dark creatures?" He swallowed hard. Reaching within his emerald green robes, he withdrew a handful of papers. "I did some digging. Here. Look at these."

I took the papers he offered and scanned them quickly, frowning.

"What *are* these?" I looked up at him.

"Obituaries of Natties. News articles of Natttie deaths," he replied. "I've been watching. I cross-referenced them with our records on potential psychic Specials within the Nattie world who didn't know what they were. Our records match with *all* of these."

"You mean, someone within *our* ranks is-is systematically ordering Natties to be *killed*?" I paled at the thought, my stomach twisting painfully. *Someone* had ordered her death. *Was her accident really an accident?* Anger began to bubble up within me. I'd thought I'd seen a wraith the night of her accident. I couldn't have imagined it.

"I think someone has been looking for Everly Torres for a very long time," he stated knowingly. "And I think someone we know is feeding the record information to the Cipher. They're looking for a mancer. We're in the middle of a war, General."

I let out a shaky breath at the news, trying to center myself so I could think straight. I glanced down at the news articles again. At least ten deaths of young Nattie and Special potentials. And *there*. An article on Everly and a photo of her smiling face obviously taken before she was injured.

*An accident involving a motor vehicle and pedestrian occurred Friday night around midnight at the corner of Dice Road and Garfield Road. Everly Torres, 17, was seriously injured when she was struck by a vehicle driven by Camden Murphy, 55. Torres had been walking down the street when she was struck by Murphy. Torres was rushed to the hospital with life-threatening injuries. An additional pedestrian received minor injuries and was treated and released. Camden received no injuries.*

I read the next article quickly, focusing on the important part.

*Torres, 17, is expected to live.*

"What the hell," I whispered hoarsely, dropping the papers onto my desk and rubbing my forehead in frustration and anger.

"I think it goes without saying that I'm quite concerned," my father's voice brought me back from the brink of an all-out rage. "You need to back away from the girl."

"We can't leave her alone—"

"You can. You must!" he shouted. "If they know she's the Mancer, what do you think is going to happen? Huh? They'll take her! She needs to die, General. She needs to die and *stay* dead. She could end our world if the Cipher get her."

"Then shouldn't we be doing all that's in our power to *protect* her to make sure that doesn't happen?" I countered hotly, my hands shaking with anger as we stared one another down.

"The girl is an abomination. She cannot live—"

"I *won't* let her die," I snarled back at him, on my feet and ready to fight right then.

"Don't force my hand, Son," my father's voice lowered threateningly.

"Do *not* force mine," I hissed back. We sized one another up for a moment. "What do you think will happen to *me* if she dies and all this is true? Huh? Do you think I could just go on living like I didn't lose the *one* thing in the world that was meant for me? I'm pretty sure her death would affect more than your concern for dominance! Her death might mean my own."

"Part of being a king is being able to overcome the hardships that come with it. That includes getting over the ones we love when they leave."

"There is a vast difference in dealing with things that happen beyond our control and allowing things to happen that can be prevented. In letting people die when they could be saved. Innocent people like Everly."

"I don't want innocent blood on my hands. And I don't want it on yours either," he breathed out. "But I will *not* see our kingdom fall. Let the girl go. If you want her to live, don't go to her. Let whatever is going to happen, happen. You've been marked. You brought her back and set in motion things that will be difficult to stop. But we *must* stop them for the sake of our people. You cannot love the girl. You cannot save the girl. If the dead want her, let them have her. Do *not* intervene. Perhaps, if you can handle staying away from her, we can offer her protection at Dementon until her skills are honed. Then maybe the girl will have a chance at a normal life. But if you connect with her, it's over. Do you understand?"

"You'll let her live until something kills her," I whispered, glaring at him.

"And you'll let her die should it come down to it. It's her or our entire people, General. Should you choose to disobey me, I will see to it that you are chained in the vorbex until the last breath leaves her body and she is turned to ash."

His whispered threat left me near hysterical with a fury that surpassed anything I'd ever felt before. I glared at him, my body shaking with the rage I was struggling to keep under wraps.

"To ensure your compliance," he continued, clearing his throat. "We've arranged your marriage to Amara LaCroix.

"*What?*" I roared. "Amara and I broke up. I will *not* be forced to marry her!"

"You are the next sigil! You will marry who I say—you will *love* who I say!"

"I'm free to love who I want—" I interjected angrily.

"Yes. As long as it's Amara." He stared at me before he let out a sigh. "It's for our people, Son. They need strength. They'll find it in you. You must present yourself as strong. The LaCroixs are one of the oldest, strongest families in our world. With your support, Benton will be inducted into the Order. Can I count on you, Son?"

Needing to appease my father in some way, I snatched a piece of paper from my desk and scribbled for a moment. I withdrew my dagger and pricked my finger, dripping blood onto the page to seal my vote. "Here." I thrusted the paper at him. "There's my vote."

"Thank you. This will help secure his spot. We need this."

"While I have no issues with Benton, I won't marry her." I shook my head. "I won't. I'm sorry, Father. I will *not* be you and mother. I want to *love* the person I marry. I want her to love me. I don't have that with Amara. And I never will. No matter how hard you push this. I'll give up the crown if I have to," I drew myself up to my impressive height, my voice strong. I'd give it all up. I meant what I said.

"I won't have a mancer as the mother of my grandchildren! If she lives forever, she holds our people *forever*! The Mancer is evil! An abomination! And in the Cipher hands? Our world is over!"

"Father," I interrupted him softly, reeling in my rage. "I didn't say it would be Everly."

"If the Wards are true, you won't be able to help yourself with the girl," he snapped back at me, his face red. "You need to be wed to Amara! Your head will be clearer with a wife on your arm. You'd be bonded to her, *not* the Mancer. The Mancer is dangerous outside Dementon walls. She's probably dangerous within its walls. I'm offering you a solution. If you take it, she may have a semblance of a normal life. If you don't, I'll see to it that she has no life at all. The choice is yours."

"And you say the Cipher is wicked," I snarled at him.

"I never said I wasn't, Son. I'm just the better of the two evils," he replied softly. "We're being attacked from within. I need you to keep this business with the Mancer a secret. Keep it between us. Don't tell the Order. Not until we get this sorted. And I want you to stay away from her. It was over before it began. You'll never be with the girl. I *won't* allow it."

I *never* said I was going to be with her. And the fact that he was telling me *who* I could be with was really pissing me off. I wouldn't stand for it. Then he wanted to threaten Everly? *No way.*

"Why? Because you believe in some thousand-year-old prophecy?" I bellowed. "Do you think I'm incapable of keeping myself loyal to the crown? I'm not an animal, Father! I can control my urges—"

"I won't take that chance. I'm sorry, Son. Your wedding is arranged. You *will* marry Amara. You *will* stay away from the Torres girl. And you *will* let her die if it comes to it."

"No!" I shouted. "You won't tell me—"

"Listen to me!" he shouted back, his face flaming red with anger, his eyes flashing dangerously. "Do *not* go to her. Do not save her! If you two can manage to keep your hands off one another, then she can come here and learn to exist. But don't count on her survival. Eventually, the girl will die. When that time comes, let it happen. Because if you don't, I will personally see to it that she's taken to Xanan and dealt with there. If you care for her as much as I suspect you do, then listen to me. She's the reason your mother is dead and rotting in a coffin in the royal crypt. Be an honorable man and avenge your mother. Stay away from the girl. Do you understand?"

"Yes," I growled through clenched teeth. His eyes swept over me quickly before he gave me a curt nod. He yanked open my door and slammed it closed behind him, leaving me scared for Everly and what it all meant.

# CHAPTER 24

*I* spent the following days doing hunts, trying to keep my mind clear of Everly. Desperately attempting to forget that I'd probably end up married in a year to someone I didn't love. I sent Adam and Chloe off to see if they could find out any information on the rumors my father had mentioned. So far, the only thing they could tell me was what I already knew. They *were* able to confirm the deaths from the articles. And, surprise, surprise, all the ones that had been killed weren't just psychics. They were all potential whisperers. And all had been involved in freak accidents like falls, car accidents, and even a drowning.

Everly's sadness washed over me every moment, which didn't help my mood any. I knew my father was serious. If I went to her and he found out, he'd send another chapter out to retrieve her. She'd be taken to Xanan and executed. And there wasn't shit I'd be able to do about it, even if I was her reever because I'd be held until her body was destroyed.

I was withdrawn, more so than usual. Circumstances made me ruthless, so I tore apart all the Cipher I encountered. I even sent some straight to Xanan to be dealt with. I was angry, and it was showing through.

"Damn, man," Damien whistled as I pulled my blade from the bleeding chest of a dying Cipher caster. I'd questioned him ruthlessly and couldn't get any information out of him. Even Eric had dug into his head only to come up empty. They had a way of blocking him though, so I wasn't surprised. I kicked the body away and nodded for Jared to dispose of it. "What's going on with you?"

"Nothing," I snapped, shoving my blade back into my cloak. Damien exchanged a quick look with Eric who was being unusually quiet, even for him. Even Adam, Brandon, and Jared looked at me oddly. "Sloane brought information on a haunt over on Westover." I stomped down the alley. "We're going. *Now*. Jared, be quick with the body, would you?"

"I'm trying," Jared muttered as his hands ignited in fire, and he heaved a ball of it at the body. It immediately burst into flames and turned to bits of ash before becoming nothing.

We walked down the dark alley, a few blocks from Westover, Eric and Damien flanking me.

"Shadow," Eric cleared his throat. "Man, what's going on? You haven't sent us to Everly—"

"And I won't be," I answered tightly. "That's over."

"What? *Why?* She needs to be protected," Damien protested.

"Let whatever happens, happen."

"Dude, what the hell?" Eric demanded. "Just last week you were saying how much you loved her—"

"It's *not* love. It's the Wards. And I need to let that shit go. It's not real. I need to be concentrating on our world, not her delusions." Maybe if I said it enough times, it would be true.

"You know she's not delusional!" Eric snarled angrily. "She needs you!"

"She needs to deal with it on her own. I have other things that need to be taken care of. I can't be there for her."

"Did your father say something to you about it?" Eric demanded angrily. "Is that why he was here that night?"

"Whatever conversations happen between me and the sigil are just that—between us. If you were meant to know, I'd have told you."

"You're being an asshole," Damien finally spoke, his eyes flashing. "If he's using your mother's death against you—"

He didn't get to finish his sentence because I collapsed to my knees, my chest aching. She was hurting. It tore at my very soul—the terror, pain, fear. I couldn't go to her though. *I couldn't!* She had to fight and win this on her own. If I went, it was her certain death. At least on her own, she had a chance. It was small, but it was better than anything I could offer her.

"Gen, you OK?" Brandon rushed forward, the rest of the guys surrounding me. I couldn't even manage to get the words out. I just clutched my chest, as the mark on my wrist burned.

"Shadow! Man!" Eric came down face-to-face with me. "Talk to me. Do you want me to go?"

My body trembled as my head shook no, and I swallowed hard.

*Everly. Everly. Everly.*

Her name was on repeat in my head. I was desperate to get to her. To hold her. To protect her. To save her.

*I can't! I'm protecting her by not going. I'm protecting myself and my people by not going. I'm avenging my mother. This is the first step in that! I'd be betraying her memory if Everly lived! Plus, I-I'd be killing any chance at survival that Everly has! What kind of monster am I? What's wrong with me?*

"Shadow! Answer me!" Eric shouted. I shook my head slightly at him again, my eyes burning. *Tears?* I never cried. I always held my emotions back.

"Stay with him," Eric ordered the guys.

"What are you doing?" Damien asked Eric, lifting me to my feet.

"I'm going to her since he won't." Eric glared at me before melding, his eyes glowing red. "I'm second in command, and since our fearless leader is unable to act, I'll be giving orders until he comes to his senses." He didn't wait for an answer. He disappeared into the shadows.

I couldn't say it, but I *was* grateful for him.

I silently cursed all the confusing emotions in my body as my friends tried to get me steady on my feet. It was torture wanting two different worlds.

# CHAPTER 25

*I* lay in bed with a killer headache the next morning. I hadn't heard back from Eric. It would be fruitless trying to get the headache to go away, so I showered and went downstairs to find Damien and Sloane arguing over who ate the last of the bread.

"Every time I want a damn sandwich, there's no bread!" Damien shouted.

"And what the hell do you want me to do about it?" Sloane shot back, her dark eyes flashing angrily. "The milk's always gone! But you don't see me complaining!"

"Bull! You threw the carton at me last week!"

"I wasn't complaining! I was making a point!"

"And what point was that?" Damien demanded.

"That you suck!"

"OK, guys," I sighed tiredly. "Chill."

Sloane folded her arms over her chest and glared at Damien. He shook his head and flopped down on the couch.

"Where's Eric?" I asked.

"Not here," Damien grunted. "He never came back last night."

"Who's not here?" Amara asked, coming into the room.

"Eric," Sloane answered, sitting on the opposite end of the couch from Damien.

"He was here earlier," Amara tossed her hair over her shoulder as she went to the kitchen. "Are we seriously out of bread again?" She let out a frustrated sigh and came back into the living room.

"I know," Damien agreed. "Never any bread."

"So walk down to the shop and get some!" I yelled, causing everyone to flinch. "Amara, did Eric say anything?"

"Not really." She shrugged. "He seemed tired. And upset. He was only here for a few minutes. Making a lot of noise, as he slammed things around in the weapons room." Her eyes slid over me quickly. "Do you have him out there with your *girlfriend* or something?"

"She's *not* my girlfriend," I snapped. "In fact, all *that* is over. I'm done with it."

"Good to know," Eric said, coming into the commons through the front door. His face was sour—his usual bright blue eyes dark, his mouth turned down into a deep frown.

"Hey." I cleared my throat.

"We need to talk. Now." He didn't wait for me to answer. Instead, he marched to my office. I followed him and closed the door behind me.

"What?" I asked going to my desk and sitting on the edge of it.

"Do you want to know what happened?"

"No." I shook my head, swallowing hard. That was a lie. It was eating me up inside to know.

"Really?" He looked at me skeptically.

"Really." I cleared my throat and stared stonily at him.

"You're ridiculous," Eric snorted disgustedly at me. "I'm not going off mission. I'm going to keep checking on her." He went to the door when I didn't say anything. "Oh, and in case you really cared, she was attacked by a wraith last night. It was able to possess her for a moment. She stabbed herself. She was in the hospital. But you don't care, right?"

He didn't wait for me to answer. He slammed the door closed behind him, leaving me there nearly vomiting. *My Everly.*

# CHAPTER 26

$\mathcal{E}$ ric wouldn't talk to me. From that point on, he dedicated himself to watching over Everly. For nearly two weeks, we didn't speak. I wanted to tell him I was thankful, but the prideful creature within me wouldn't let me to do it. Instead, I worked harder taking out the Cipher and hunting dark creatures. I threw myself so deeply into it I was hardly at home, always out there. Maybe deep down I thought the more I sent back, the more I killed, the safer Everly would be. I was seeking redemption in everything I did with her on my mind. I wasn't living up to all the promises I'd made to her. I was the worst Reever. I left my second in command to tend to her, knowing if I got too close I'd lose myself in her. Knowing my father would make good on his word and have her killed. That couldn't happen. So, this was all I had to offer her. Killing for her. Many of the traitors I encountered were sent directly to Xanan. I wanted them to suffer. They were out to get her and didn't deserve my pity.

And to top it all off, I still had to figure out how to get out of my arranged marriage to Amara. I hadn't even bothered talking to her about it. The thought of being forced to marry someone I didn't love left me sick to my stomach. Not that Amara wasn't a good girl. She just wasn't *my* girl. And I didn't want her to be. Not anymore. I'd rather be alone than marry someone I didn't love. Marriage had never even crossed my mind. In fact, if someone had asked me about it, I'd have said absolutely not ever. Even though I knew realistically, at some point I'd have to, just so I could keep my royal line going. But in the back of my mind I'd hoped by then I'd found someone I could love. Honestly, I'd never thought myself capable of love before Everly. When she came back into my life, she confused everything I thought I knew and what I believed myself capable of.

All the worry and stress kept me hunting all through the summer months. The end of it came quicker than I wanted. Another school year was upon us. And I still didn't have any word on whether Everly would be coming to Dementon. I hadn't been able to dig up anything else on who the mole was in our ranks.

Eric was still avoiding me. I'd only seen him in glimpses over the past weeks. Whenever I asked Damien about him, he only shrugged and said he hadn't talked to him much either. I was in the dark about her. It was driving me crazy, but I knew she was safe if Eric was that dedicated to her.

On the flipside, I couldn't help but wonder if he'd shown himself to her. If maybe in some offhand way, he'd forged a friendship with her, or any sort of relationship. He was replacing me as her protector. The feeling left me sick. Sick in my guts. Sick in my heart. And sick in my soul. But if she were to want anyone, Eric would be a good choice.

I was overthinking things. I knew I was. But I couldn't seem to help myself. I needed to talk to Eric.

"You seen Eric?" I asked Jared as I came into the room.

"Sorry, Gen. I haven't seen him all week. You must have him out on something big."

"Yeah," I grunted. Grabbing my cloak, I went outside, walking in the direction of Headmaster Brighton's. I knocked on his door, deciding if I couldn't find Eric, Brighton would be the next best thing.

"Come in," he called out. I opened the door and stepped inside. Ceres, Brighton's hellhound, walked up and gave my hand a sniff before deciding I wasn't worth the bark. He sauntered back to his fluffy bed and flopped down, keeping his eyes trained on me sleepily.

Moving deeper into the room, I found Brighton seated at his desk pouring over paperwork. "What can I help you with?"

"I want to know how Everly Torres is progressing." I cleared my throat, standing in the center of the room feeling awkward. Or maybe it was guilty.

"Well..." He pulled his nose out of his papers and looked at me. "She isn't."

"What?" I frowned, stepping closer to his desk. "What do you mean?"

"She claims the voices are gone. She says she hasn't seen anything since the night of the possession, which I'm sure you heard about."

"Really?" I asked, frowning more deeply. This could be a good thing. *A great thing!* She could have just had that injury, and it made her sensitive. Maybe over time she'd healed. I'd read articles where people with head injuries started seeing things others couldn't.

"Really." He nodded. "Of course, she's lying. She ate the butter mint without an issue. She's definitely a Special."

"Oh." My heart fell. For a moment there, I envisioned her free of our world. Happy. Safe. Butter mint was used to determine if a Nattie was a Special. Of course, to give a Nattie a butter mint also meant they may become quite ill if they weren't actually a Special. We only employed the tactic when we didn't have a doubt they were one of us. "So what's the plan? Are you able to get her here?"

"Do you *want* her here?" Headmaster Brighton countered, raising an eyebrow at me. "I was under the impression that you didn't care any longer when you didn't show up for the possession. I gathered that information from Mr. Craft as well."

"It's not like that," I muttered, looking away. I looked down at Ceres as she nibbled at a bone in her bed with gusto, slobber everywhere.

"I *know* what it's like. The sigil came to you. I was outside when he arrived." Brighton rubbed his eyes. "Listen. This is what I know. She's a strong girl. Resilient... but terrified. I have her drugged twenty-four-seven in an effort to bring her some comfort. The girl is living in a haze and doesn't know if she's coming or going. It dulls the dead for her, it deadens—excuse my words—her senses, so she doesn't see much of anything until the meds begin to wear off."

"But she's fine?" I ventured, swallowing hard and glancing back to Brighton.

"No." He shook his head with a sigh. "She's teetering on the edge of madness, General. She's only a step away from tumbling over. But that's what we want, isn't it? For her to fall? Then we can get her here under the guise of a specialty institute. Or has the plan changed?"

"No," I answered fiercely. "That's still the plan. I want her here by any means necessary."

"Even if it means it hurts her?" he asked, raising an eyebrow at me.

"I don't want her hurt," I replied softly, the ache of wanting to keep her safe very real.

"Well, I don't see another way around it. She's going to have to hurt. Besides, if it's too much, you'll just come for her, right?"

"No." I shook my head, swallowing past the lump in my throat. "I won't."

"What?" His eyebrows shot up, his eyes wide.

"I won't come for her." My voice shook as I said the words I hated, "If she dies, she dies."

# CHAPTER 27

*J* wasn't sleeping. I wasn't eating. I was so sick with worry, I couldn't focus, and I'd nearly been gutted by a goblin on a hunt. Thankfully, it had only resulted in a deep wound to my abdomen. A wound that took both me and Brandon to heal.

I was so lost in my thoughts as I sat at my desk in my office peering out the window on the darkened school grounds as night descended, that I didn't notice Eric slip into the room.

"You look like shit," his voice dragged me out of my reverie—all my thoughts on Everly.

"Hey," I said in monotone, looking at him.

"Hey." He sat down in the chair across from me. As he regarded me he remained silent. He looked exhausted. His usually vibrant blue eyes were dull and tired, dark circles rimming them. His blond hair was a mess on his head. I watched him, a surge of sadness flowing through me. It was my fault. All of it. And no one could hate me more than I hated myself for what he was going through. What I knew she had to be going through. Finally, he cleared his throat. "We should probably talk, man."

Sighing, I nodded, knowing we had to.

"Listen, Ever isn't well. That beautiful girl you showed me? She's

143

gone. The light is dead in her eyes. She doesn't eat. She hardly interacts with people. She's just a shell of the person she once was. I spoke to Brighton. He told me she needs to crack in order to get her here. But, man…" He shook his head sadly, his blond hair falling forward. "At what *cost*? At this rate, she's going to die from either a sickness or heartbreak. I'm not sure which will take her first."

I ground my teeth at his words, not saying anything.

"I get that you're following orders. And that you think you're somehow avenging your mother's death by staying away from her. I understand. I *do*. But Shadow, she's your other half. You're destined to be with her. How can you just sit back and not protect her? To know she's suffering, and all those words you said to her were a lie? She calls your name out while she sleeps—which isn't often since she's terrified to close her eyes. I've been with her for weeks, watching, listening, as she searches for you. I don't even think she knows she's looking for you."

"I can't help her," I whispered sadly. "I want to. God knows, I do."

"Then just go to her!"

"No." I shook my head, my vision blurring. "You don't understand."

"Then tell me because I want to. I want to know why my *best* friend who was clearly in love with this girl, now keeps his distance *knowing* how much she's suffering."

"The sigil has forbidden it."

"Since when have you *ever* listened to your father?" Eric demanded, his blue eyes flashing angrily.

"Since he threatened to have her killed and me held back so I wouldn't be able to save her," I answered in a low whisper. "Since he reminded me she's the reason my mother is dead."

"What?" Eric sounded sick. "Your mom is dead because a *vamp* killed her. Not because of some scared twelve-year-old girl! And really, *who* would he send? *We're* the best. Any other chapter sent to her would get decimated. You know that, man!"

Grinding my teeth, I looked away. I knew he was making a valid point, but I didn't want to see it. Besides, attaching another Conexus group would basically be like attacking the Order. We'd be charged with treason.

"He's worried she'll control me. That my rule as the next sigil will be tainted because of her. He's arranged my marriage to Amara," I said the words sourly. Angrily. Bitterly. "He thinks if I'm married, bonded, I won't go to Everly. That I'll remain loyal to m-my *wife*," I spat, hating the word. It was even hard to say.

"Jesus, Shadow! Why didn't you say something? Does Amara know?"

"I don't know if she knows. I'm assuming she doesn't or she'd have said something to me about it already."

"So, you're just going to let Ever suffer?"

"What choice do I have?" I roared, angry at myself for being so weak against my father's wishes. "Maybe you'll slip and not be there, and she'll finally get to rest in peace." Those words were incredibly painful to say.

"The Shadow I knew wouldn't stand for it. He wouldn't let the girl he loved be hurt. He'd be there for her!" Eric countered heatedly. "He wouldn't wish for her death!"

"I'm doing *this*, so she doesn't get hurt!" I explained passionately. "I'd rather she hurt a little bit than *die*, but if she must die, then I have to let her go! I've promised to stay away from her. If I do, she gets to live. She might be able to have a semi-normal life once she's brought to Dementon. If she and I don't connect, nothing happens. Don't you understand? You think I've stopped caring, man. But it's just the opposite! I care too much! It's killing me too! And it's not just that!" I launched into telling him what my father had told me about a mole in our ranks. Eric visibly paled.

"*Who* would betray us like that?" he asked.

"We don't know. I've been questioning every creature I capture. No one is talking." I rubbed my eyes. "I wish I knew."

We both fell silent, staring at one another. My head and heart were in turmoil for completely different reasons.

Finally, Eric spoke, "I don't care about the mole right now. We'll figure that out like we always do. Right now, she needs you, Shadow.

145

No one will know if you show her hope by appearing and helping her every now and then. I have to work hard to stay hidden from her. I've been slaying wraiths left and right that try entering her house."

"Why do *you* care so much about her?" I asked softly, voicing the fears buried inside of me.

He chuckled softly, sadly, his eyes downcast as he stared at his hands.

"I'm all she has left now that you're gone," he finally said, his words barely above a whisper. "I couldn't live with myself if I didn't try. It's not in my nature to back down from anything. And I won't start with this. I don't care if the Order fears her. Or if your father does. Or if *you* do. I don't even care if you hate her, however undeserved that hatred is. I *know* she's a good person and deserves to be saved. If we help her, she may not become something we fear. She may be exactly what we *need* to end this war with the Cipher. And for that reason alone, I'll fight for her."

# CHAPTER 28

*E*ric was right. Everly was the best hope we had for ending the war with the Cipher. At the very least, we needed to keep her out of their hands, because if they got her they'd try to get her to create an army to take over our world. If she was in as bad of shape as he said, I had to help her. I just wouldn't tell my father, and I knew I could count on Eric, Damien, and the rest of my crew to keep it quiet.

On the other hand, I knew if I saw her, I'd break. She'd crack me open like an egg, my guts pouring out around me as I tried to keep my distance from her. A day later, I was still contemplating all of it, warring with myself just to pop in and check on her, when that familiar warmness rushed over me. She was in trouble. I rubbed my chest, my teeth clenched.

*Why was I hesitating? Why was I leaving my best friend to take care of her?* She wasn't Eric's responsibility. I was being an idiot. Letting out a frustrated growl and vowing I'd only do it this *one* time, I melded into the shadows and followed the pull in my gut to her.

Then I was standing outside her school. And there was Eric, fighting with five carrion on the front steps.

*What the hell was happening?*

I rushed forward and drew my sword, slashing through two of the carrion.

"She needs you! Go! I've got this!" he shouted out, his brow wet with sweat. I nodded, knowing I needed to hurry because there were more carrion ambling their way across the grounds toward him. I rushed into the building and went straight to where the attraction was coming from.

I drew in a sharp breath as I entered the cafeteria to find Everly on her butt pushed up against a table, her green eyes wide and terrified as an inkling, a dog-like creature from the void, lay ready to pounce on her. Rushing forward, I wielded my blade and plunged it through the creature, turning it to nothing but bits of dust and ash.

Our eyes locked on one another, and my heart lurched. She looked like she was falling apart. Gone was the girl from before. My Everly had lost so much weight. She was gaunt and thin, her hair limp, her once vibrant eyes now dull in comparison to how bright and beautiful they once were. She was tiny and vulnerable as she stared at me. I could almost hear everything she was thinking, and it broke my heart.

*"I'm so sorry!"* I screamed out in my head, fighting the urge to just go to her and take her into my arms and hold her forever. I'd let her down. She was breaking because of *me*. The argument still raged on in my head—I was doing this *for* her, not *to* her.

I stiffened as Dylan got to his feet and went to her, drawing her attention away from me. It didn't last long. Her gaze found mine again, and I knew she had to be fighting the same war I was. She wanted to come to me just as badly as I wanted to go to her. In my mind that only proved how strong of a link we had to one another. Being near her was a *very* bad idea.

"We need to get you to the nurse's office," Dylan said gently to her.

"I-I," she stammered looking to Dylan quickly before peering back at me. I stood unmoving, anger resonating out of me as Dylan placed his hands on her tenderly. He started tugging her away from me. I wanted to end that guy. He'd hurt her. And he still wanted her. She was vulnerable!

*She's not yours. You gave her up, remember?*

I gave her a curt nod as Dylan pulled her away, confusion and unspoken words on her lips as she let him. Turning on my heel, I disappeared through the cafeteria wall.

I had some carrion to kill.

## CHAPTER 29

"Is she safe?" Eric asked as I rushed outside and rammed my blade through a carrion at his back.

"For now," I grunted, slashing through two more. Eric dispatched the final one with his knife, and we both stood panting on the steps.

"What's 'for now' mean?" Eric asked, pushing his hair out of his eyes as he stuffed his sword back into his cloak.

"There." I nodded as the doors opened. We both melded into the shadow of a nearby tree and watched as Dylan helped Everly out to his car. Her eyes were glassy with tears, her small body shaking. "She's leaving with him."

We watched as Dylan left the parking lot with her.

"I'll go," Eric said calmly. "I know your patience is thin. I don't want you to do something you'll regret."

"Thank you," I said, clearing my throat. He knew me well. He knew if I saw Dylan touch her I'd come alive and rip his head off. "Do what you have to do, no matter what. Promise?"

"You have my word, brother," Eric answered solemnly.

"I know. And I'm sorry... About everything."

Eric gave me a nod before disappearing. Sighing, I melded back to

151

Dementon, once again sick with worry. *When would that go away?* I knew the answer to that. Once Everly was here where she could be watched. Where she could be safe.

# CHAPTER 30

*S*omething was wrong. Eric hadn't come back. He hadn't reported to me. Everly's distress washed over me in waves, but I stayed away, knowing Eric would deal with it.

"What's eating you?" Damien asked, biting into his sandwich as he flopped down on the couch in the commons room.

"Eric isn't back yet."

"You two kiss and make up?" Damien raised an inquisitive eyebrow at me.

"Yeah, douche." I rolled my eyes at him and then told him the story about earlier.

"I'm glad. I was worried about you two."

"Why?" I asked, leaning against the fireplace mantle.

"Because Eric was becoming a little *too* invested in this. I figured if he hadn't already shown himself to her, he would soon. And *if* he did, there'd be a very good reason for it."

"Like?" I frowned.

"I'm not saying shit." Damien took another bite of his sandwich. "I just know you aren't the only one who cares about her. I mean, how could he *not*? He's been by her side for weeks now while you deal with your crap."

I didn't say anything, his words making my stomach roll. He was right. Eric *was* invested in this. I didn't blame him. He was a good friend and soldier. He did it for both reasons. I knew he cared for her too. *How could he not? She was strong and smart and beautiful... She was amazing.* Damien was right. But I trusted Eric with my life. I knew he'd never make a move on Everly. He wasn't that kind of guy. He knew what she meant to me. How I felt about her.

"It is weird he's not back yet." Damien stuffed the last bite of his sandwich in his mouth. "He's been coming back around this time to grab dinner. We should probably go look for him."

I nodded, going to grab my cloak. I was just reaching for it when the common room door burst open, and Adam entered half carrying Eric in.

"What the hell happened?" I demanded, rushing to help. Damien scrambled off the couch as Adam and I pulled Eric to it and laid him down. His eyes rolled back in his head, and his breathing was deep and labored. Sweat dampened his brow, and his skin was pale.

"He stitched," Damien murmured, staring down at him.

"Get Brandon," I commanded, going down to my knees and placing my hands on either side of Eric's head. Adam rushed off to get Brandon, leaving me and Damien with Eric. He must have done a huge stitch. Whenever he stitched normally, he got very weak, leading him to have to sleep for days. *This* time was bigger than anything he'd ever done before. Hastily, I pushed my healing energy into him. He let out a groan, his body twitching.

"God." I breathed out as Brandon rushed into the room.

"What happened?" he demanded, falling to his knees beside me.

"He must have done a huge stitch," I answered, worrying over why. I had to get him back, so he could tell me what happened. I didn't feel anything coming from Everly, so whatever he'd done, must have worked. She must be safe. *For now.*

"Damien?" I tore my eyes away from Eric.

"Yeah?"

"Go to her," I whispered. He nodded and disappeared without a word.

I placed my hands over Eric's chest, and Brandon put his on either side of his head. Together, we both pushed forward, sending as much healing as we could at Eric. When we'd drained ourselves, we stepped back and surveyed him.

His lashes fluttered for a moment before his eyes opened.

"Welcome back, man," I murmured.

"Shit," he groaned reaching out weakly to rub his head, his eyes heavy.

"You OK? What happened?" I asked.

Eric looked from Adam to Brandon then back to me. I nodded, understanding. I didn't need to say anything. The guys took the hint and left the room.

"Her father. She contacted him. She wanted answers. Then he tried to convince her to kill herself. When she refused, he came at her with a *knife*. I-I showed myself to her, man. She knows me now... But I saved her. I'm sorry."

"Don't be." I patted his arm. "You did what you had to do."

"I didn't know what else to do. I-I went into that diner as me. Not a shadow. Not a shade. Just *me*. She needs to know us. I don't want to hide from her anymore." He struggled to swallow, his breathing uneven. I frowned at my friend as a tear slid from his eye. He quickly wiped it away. In all the years I'd known Eric, I'd *never* seen him cry. "She needs you. She's so scared. I wanted to follow her to make sure she made it. But I-I couldn't. I was too weak. Go to her, man. Let her know you're there."

"I will," I agreed, my throat tight. "Will you be OK?"

"Yeah." He nodded weakly. "I'm just beat. I'll stay here until I get more energy. Don't worry about me. Just go see her."

I rose to my feet and drew my cloak on.

"Thank you," I said, before I melded.

# CHAPTER 31

*D*amien was outside her bedroom door when I arrived.
*"Thank God you're here,"* he said, his voice in my head as we both stood as shadows. *"I sent a lost one to Xanan in my voidbox. It was in her dining room."*

*"Was that all of them?"*

*"For now,"* Damien answered tightly.

*"Is she not well?"* I asked, glancing at her closed door.

*"She fought with her mom. She's just upset. How's Eric?"*

*"Tired, but alive."* I nodded.

*"Good. He had me worried,"* Damien sighed. *"Can we just end this, man? Can't you just go to the Order and get this over with? Get her to Dementon. Classes start soon. I'm sick of worrying."*

*"You worry?"* I looked at him in surprise.

*"Believe it or not, I've been worrying about this chick since you brought me here. She's a good girl, man. She deserves to be happy. So, let's make it happen, OK?"*

*"OK."* I smiled stepping forward. But it left my lips as I felt the tug in my chest for her. She was so sad.

*"I'll wait here,"* Damien said.

I nodded and entered her room.

She was sitting on her bed, her legs off the floor and tucked safely under her. Her dark hair spilled forward, and her body trembled as she sobbed softly. My heart broke watching her.

"What do you want from me?" she asked, lifting her head up, but keeping her eyes squeezed closed as if she was afraid to look at me. Without thought, I went to her, collapsing to my knees. I reached out for her and brushed her tears away, my heart beating madly in my chest as I touched her warm skin. She opened her eyes, eyes filled with sadness, and stared at me. It unnerved me, this beautiful girl. My own tears fell as I gazed back at her. *Oh, how I wanted to kiss those sweet, warm lips and hold her.* To whisper that everything would be OK. I wanted her to know that she was mine and that I was hers.

"Why did you save me if I'm meant to die?" she choked out, more tears falling.

I couldn't bear the thought of her thinking she was meant to die. The words gutted me, the same words I'd been thinking for ages now. Reaching forward, I pressed a finger to her soft lips, not wanting her to utter such things. They were ugly falling from her mouth. I shook my head at her.

*No. No, you were* not *meant to die!* I wanted to scream it as loudly as I could. Instead, I took her small hand in mine and placed it over my heart. Then I placed my hand over her heart. Our hearts nearly beat in time with one another. She looked at me curiously as my heart hammered beneath her warm fingers. Emotions flickered across her face as she worked through something. If only I could read her mind. But I imagined she was connecting the dots, remembering me from the night she almost died. She probably wanted to know why I had a heartbeat. Her eyes filled with wonder. I bet she thought I was one of *them* this entire time. I knew it. I longed to tell her everything. But I knew I couldn't. But in my heart, I had this sense of peace that she at least understood I wasn't like those that longed to harm her. It was a bittersweet moment.

"This doesn't make any sense," she murmured. Inching forward, I rested my forehead against hers and breathed out slowly. I wanted her to know that I wasn't one of them. I *needed* her to understand that I wasn't a monster who haunted her. That I was real. That I lived. I breathed. My heart beat. *For her.*

When I pulled away from her, it felt like I was leaving a part of me behind. I hoped she'd keep it dear to her heart. Reluctantly, I got to my feet and backed away. It was one of the hardest things I'd ever had to do, and that included staying away from her.

"Where are you going?" she asked worriedly, reaching out for me. I nearly ran back to her, but I held it together. Now wasn't the time. I had to keep her safe. And that meant leaving her. I couldn't risk the Order—my father—finding out that I'd been there with her.

*God, I needed her! I wanted her!* I'd never felt that way about *anything* in my entire life. It was a painful, breathless feeling once I let it in. And I hated it, so I pushed it away, stuffing it back into the box I reserved for it in my heart.

"Why won't you talk to me!" her voice was desperate, her hand still stretching out to me. Sadly, I bowed my head at her, knowing I had to go. I melded away, leaving the sound of her sad voice calling out after me.

"I'll be back, Everly," I murmured through the shadows. "I promise."

# CHAPTER 32

"I'm proud of you, man." Damien clapped me on the shoulder as we walked—yes, walked—down the street. I didn't want to go back to Dementon just yet. I needed some time away.

"You shouldn't be," I commented, looking up to the moon. "I wasn't going to come. But then I saw the lengths Eric went through to keep her safe."

"You're worried he's falling for her," Damien replied keenly. I glanced at him with a half-smile—a sad one.

"Yeah, I am," I answered. "He's better for her than I am. *He* could be with her. If I am, it could be disastrous."

"What are you going to do if she comes to Dementon?"

"I don't know," I answered honestly.

"Look, you'd be a damn fool to *not* notice what the girl looks like. She's beautiful. If she comes to Dementon, guys are going to want her. I know that should be the least of our worries—your worries—but hear me out. If *you* can't be with her, don't you want someone you trust to take care of her? Not some Special trying to impress her with his fancy tricks."

"What are you trying to say?" I asked, stopping on the sidewalk and turning to face him.

"Talk to Eric. He can befriend her. Maybe show her a good time. If she's kept interested in him, she won't have eyes for anyone else. And you'll feel good knowing she's hanging with someone who's a good dude."

"You want me to set my best friend up with the girl I care about— the girl *I'm* meant to be with? What do I do if she falls in love with him? Or him with her? How is that a good idea?"

"Not to date. Maybe just as a male figure to keep her mind occupied. A close friend. She won't have anyone once she starts at Dementon. You *know* Eric. You know he'd back down if asked. And if the Order thinks she has interests elsewhere, maybe they won't ride you so hard about her. And by Order, I mean your father. She'd be even safer. He'd see her content with Eric and leave you alone about her. Not to mention maybe then you won't be forced into marrying Amara. Plus, if you really don't want to be with her, then maybe something *could* happen with Eric. God knows Eric could use a girl in his life. And you know he'd take care of her. It could really work out."

I rolled his words over in my mind. He made a lot of sense. And as painful as it was to admit, maybe he was right. It would keep her safe. But I'd fall apart if she fell in love with him. It was a dangerous game to play, but then again, so was the alternative. And Damien was right —I wasn't going to be with her as painful as that was. Everly deserved to be happy, that much I knew. Eric might make her happy. It was worth a shot.

"Do you think he'd do it?" I asked softly as we started to walk again.

"I honestly don't know. You know Eric. He doesn't say much. But I think if he knows what's at stake, he'll say yes."

"I'm surprised you didn't offer yourself up." I chuckled quietly.

"I'll do it if Eric won't," he answered with a shrug of his broad shoulders. "I just figured he'd be better at it than me. I'm not really good at keeping chicks around. I tend to piss them off."

"You *are* pretty terrible." We shared a laugh.

"You going to do it?" Damien asked after a few moments.

"Yeah, I think so," I murmured. "I know she's going to need a friend, and Eric would be a good one. Plus, he's shown himself to her already, so she'll probably accept his friendship knowing he protected her."

"See? All the pieces are falling into place. Now, you'll just have to figure out how you're going to work it with all those rules you have about Conexus not associating with anyone at Dementon but our group."

"Training." I nodded. "He'll be her trainer. She has to be trained in combat at Dementon. It's a requirement. I'll make sure he's assigned to her."

"There ya go, Gen. See? You've got it all worked out."

"I hardly think so," I said sadly, my throat tight as I thought about the repercussions. It was worth it though. I knew it was.

# CHAPTER 33

*I* went directly to Eric's room when I returned to our house. He was propped up in bed, wearing his pajamas and staring at the wall in front of him.

"Hey, can I come in?" I asked, poking my head into his room.

"Yeah, man." He glanced at me and shifted in bed.

"How are you feeling?" I walked in and sat down in the chair next to his bed.

"I've been better." He chuckled. "That was rough. I've never done such a big stitch. Didn't even know I was capable of something so large."

"Strange what we realize we can do when we don't have another choice." I laughed softly at the irony of it.

"Yeah," he commented lightly, wincing. "I think I'm going to be out of commission for tonight. Are you going to go keep an eye on her?"

"No." I shook my head. His face instantly darkened, and I rushed on, "Damien is going to go back after he eats." Eric relaxed in his bed, his mouth still turned down in a frown.

"So… What else did you do at the diner?" I asked after a moment.

"Huh?"

"I know you've done big stitches before. What *else* did you do?"

He looked at me guiltily before speaking, "I wiped her father's mind. All of them. Everyone at the diner has no recollection of me, Everly, or her father."

"*Completely?*" I frowned. I knew Eric had been practicing with wipes, but I didn't know if he'd gotten better at them. Last I knew, he was only able to erase small bits of memory, but they seemed to come back to the person only hours later.

"Just of the event." He swallowed hard, not looking at me. "I wanted to kill him. I had my blade at his throat. You told me all the stories of how awful he was to her. And he was stitched. I could've done anything to him, Shadow. *Anything.* I looked down at the table and saw the photo Everly had. She was her on her dad's lap. They looked happy. Normal. But behind them were all sorts of wanderers. The dead. I-I just knew I couldn't kill him. He was haunted, maybe even possessed. I saw that photo and realized that at some point she loved him and him, her. Who am I to take that from her? He needs help, not death. But that doesn't change the fact that I hate the man. If he comes near her again, I *will* end him," his voice was hard.

"How do you know the wipe worked?" I asked, the passion in his voice making my stomach clench.

"Because," he sighed. "Something happened in there. It was like something clicked inside my head. Maybe it was her presence. Maybe she can make Specials around her stronger. I just don't know. I can't explain it. I just *know*. It's an overwhelming feeling I get."

I nodded. I understood overwhelming feelings.

"So what's the plan?" Eric asked, his voice shaking slightly. "What are we going to do with her?"

"That's actually one of the reasons I came to see you." I cleared my throat and looked down at my hands, Everly's beautiful green eyes flashing in my mind, making my heart ache. "I have a mission for you."

# CHAPTER 34

"*Y*ou want me to befriend her?" Eric frowned, sitting up in his bed and staring at me.

I quickly explained the reasoning behind it, and Eric sat shaking his head.

"No. I won't do it," he declared, his voice soft. "And not because I don't want to help her... because I do want to more than anything. It's because getting close to her would hurt you, man. Our friendship could suffer if I became friends with her. I don't want that. I know how you feel about her. Even just being her friend would cause you pain. We've been friends *way* too long. I can't."

"Listen, you're my first choice. If you won't do it, I'll assign Damien. And if Damien fails, I'll assign Brandon. Or Adam. Or Jared. Or *any* other male we have in our chapter. But it will be one of you—"

"Why can't it be you?" Eric snapped, his blue eyes flashing angrily. "She's *your* girl! *Your* destiny! You want me to befriend her? And then what? Huh? How do I get away from our members being mad about me socializing outside *our* circle? How do I keep all our secrets if she starts asking? How do I draw the line between friendship a-and more? We have *rules* for a reason!"

"I know what I'm asking of you is insane," I said softly, my eyes downcast. "But I trust you, Eric. I trust you with her. I *know* you'll do right by me. More won't happen. You'll just be her friend. Her guide during this."

"But I'd be doing wrong by her," he countered. "I'd be there under false pretenses."

"They aren't false pretenses. If you didn't care about her you'd never have kept protecting her," I argued. He shook his head, a muscle thrumming along his jaw as he glared at me. This had to work.

"My father has arranged my marriage to Amara. Damien is right. If we can make it look like Ever has interest elsewhere, it could get him off my back. It could buy me some time until I figure out what to do. Plus, it's for her own good." I finally looked at him. "I know you care about her. I can see it in your face, hear it in your voice, and even tell by your actions."

"Of course, I care! But I'm like you, man! I don't even know the girl. I've spoken to her *once*. You and I are the same page here! How the hell would I even get her to trust me enough to hang out with me? And where the hell would I hang out with her at? It's not like I'm some normal dude at school. It'll put her in the spotlight if she's seen with me. I probably seriously freaked her out in the diner. I didn't tell her shit about anything other than she needed to run! Plus, you know I suck with women. The longest relationship I've ever had was a month with Kylie Newmar before she transferred to Rover Heights. And that was a secret relationship because I was in Conexus. If I couldn't make that work, an *actual* relationship, what the hell makes you think I can make this work, and it's just a friendship? I'd still be sneaking around with her, just like with Kylie, and for God's sake, she's *your* girl. Do you know how freaking awkward this would be for me? I don't want you hating me because I get close to her. This just isn't going to work." He let out a deep sigh before continuing, "I hate that you're being forced into marrying Amara. I know you don't love her, and for what it's worth, I'm sorry. It's not fair. You deserve to choose, man. I get where you're coming from on me hanging out with Ever when she gets here. I *do*. I know what it could mean for you."

"Yeah, it sucks," I mumbled. "But I'm more worried about Ever than me right now. Believe me, I've thought about everything you've just said. You're right. Neither of us has anything with her—"

"Except you, her freaking *Reever*!"

"She's just a girl to me. That's all she'll ever be." The lie was painful. God, she was so much more than *just a girl* to me. "She and I won't ever be together, Eric. And she's going to need a friend. She knows you. She'll trust you. I'm not asking this of you as your general. I'm asking as your friend. Please help me?"

"I-I can't, man."

"Eric..." I sat forward. "You care about her."

"Of course I care! I'm not some heartless asshole! I also care about my mom's cat, Mittens! Does that mean I'm cut out to be its vet? No!"

"You care just a little bit more about her than you do a damn cat, Eric," I said gently. He didn't say anything, his mouth twisted into a deep frown. "Please do this."

"I don't want to hurt her."

"If it keeps her safe—" I argued.

"It doesn't. It'll break her heart if she finds out none of it was real. That I wasn't really her friend. And I saw the whole ordeal with her and that Dylan dweeb firsthand. I don't want any part of this. Don't make me," he said fiercely, his blue eyes wavering as he stared at me.

"Fine." I nodded, knowing I wasn't going to let it go. Tonight, I'd let him win. I think he knew it too when I got to my feet. "But it wouldn't be fake. You know you already care. It would be real. We'll talk about it tomorrow. Sleep on it."

"I really hate you right now."

"I know," I said softly, closing the door behind me as I left his room. "I really hate me right now, too."

# CHAPTER 35

"*S*hadow, there's a fire message for you," Sloane greeted me as I descended the stairs after my visit with Eric. She handed me the charred piece of parchment, and I snatched it out of her hand.

*You are being summoned to the council to stand before the Order. Your presence is required immediately. You are required to bring your first and second in command. We will be expecting you.*

*Signed,*

*Sir Wesley R. Hawthorne, Grand Sigil, First Degree Conexus Elite, First Chair of the Order*

"Shit!" I hissed as the parchment sizzled, the flames licking it until it was reduced to ash.

"Is it bad?" Sloane ventured.

"I don't know. Get Damien."

Sloane scampered off as Amara entered the room.

"Trouble in paradise?" She sneered as she glanced at my face.

"I need you to accompany me to a meeting with the Order. Eric's too ill." I ignored her jab.

"Are you asking me or telling me?" Her hands came to rest on her slender hips as she surveyed me with narrowed eyes.

"I'm commanding you as your general. Get your things. We leave at once." I didn't have time for her crap. Something was going on, and we needed to get there. Fast. I looked over my shoulder as Damien entered the room, a slice of pizza in his hands.

"We've been summoned to appear before the Order. We need to go. Now," I said.

"Why do they always do this shit?" he grumbled. "I just got my dinner!"

"Tough luck. You can eat it when you get back," I said, wrapping my black cloak around me. Amara was already dressed and ready to go. I gave her a nod of approval which was met with a roll of her eyes.

"If I get to come back," he mumbled, handing Sloane his slice of pizza. She stuffed it into her mouth and winked at him.

"You're such a tease," he sighed, wrapping his cloak around himself. "You better not eat all of the pizza. I'll kick your ass so hard if there's none left when I get back."

"Ooh, I'm so scared." She rolled her eyes, dancing away from him. He looked like he wanted to tug the pizza out of her hand. I put my hand on his shoulder and led him to the basement to the portal.

"Did they say what was so important?" Damien asked with a sigh as we stood in front of the portal.

"No." I shook my head, placing my hand on the emblem to activate it. It glowed brightly, the edge of the city in view through the gateway. "But let's try to stay positive."

"Easy for you to say. You probably already ate." Damien took a frustrated step into the portal leaving me behind with Amara.

We looked at one another for a moment before she spoke in a soft voice, "My father told me we're to be married."

"I won't marry you."

"I know," she answered simply. "But I also know you can't be with that ghost whisperer. So I know there's hope for us someday."

"There really isn't," I stated dryly.

"Keep telling yourself that." She chuckled softly, taking my hand in hers and pulling me through the portal to Xanan.

# CHAPTER 36

*T*here was no one there to protect Everly. The thought weighed heavily on me as we entered the Citadel and went into the Circle. The members of the Order sat waiting for us, looking just as stern as ever.

"Good evening," the sigil stated as we stood before him. "I'm impressed at your prompt response."

"And I'd be impressed if we moved this little pow-wow along," I growled.

"Do you have plans, General?" Sir Broderick asked with a raised eyebrow.

"I have raids to do. I have a school that's starting in just a few short weeks. I have to ensure the safety of the people within its walls. There is much that needs to be done. So please, say your piece so we can get on with it."

"I must say, I thought we asked for your first in command. I see you've brought your betrothed instead." My father smirked at me, making me want to punch something.

"Eric is ill. He performed a stitch earlier that left him drained. I brought Amara in his stead simply because she was there, not for any other reason," I returned.

"You speak so lowly of your future bride," Sir Mathis commented.

"We're not engaged," I shot back. "And any who claim otherwise are liars."

"Shadow, man. Chill," Damien whispered.

"The agreement I entered into with the sigil suggests otherwise," Sir LaCroix spoke up, looking from his daughter to me.

"Then perhaps the next time you decide to enter into an agreement, you should get the other people involved to actually agree to it. Amara and I have broken up. There's no room for reconciliation at this time."

"At this time?" Sir Broderick chuckled. "But there will be."

"No," I said firmly.

"We didn't drag them here for this," Sir Sangrey finally spoke up. "This whole marriage thing is something that can be hashed out at another time."

I shot him a grateful look, and he returned it with a slight nod of his head.

"We're here to discuss bringing the whisperer to Dementon," he continued. "General, Headmaster Brighton has been reporting her progress to us. It seems the girl is heavily medicated and suffering from…" He shuffled sheets of parchment before looking up at me.

I glanced at my father. His mouth was turned down into a deep frown. The Order must have voted on Everly coming to Dementon, and he lost the vote. I knew deep down he'd rather her stay as far from me as possible. "Ah here it is. Anxiety, depression, delusions, and possible suicidal tendencies. Are you aware of such things?"

"I'm aware of her depression. The others, no." I frowned. *Possible suicidal tendencies? That wraith possessed her! She didn't hurt herself.*

"Well, if Brighton says it's true, it must be." Sangrey stared at me over his glasses. "Now, I'm under the understanding that you've ceased all communication with the girl, and she is currently alone, fighting the dead and dark creatures off on her own. Is this correct?"

"Yes," I answered through gritted teeth.

"And you've agreed to not interfere should she need protecting?"

"I have." I nodded tightly. Amara shot me a quick look, a frown on her face.

The Order regarded me quietly for a moment before Sangrey continued. "We've agreed to allow the girl to attend Dementon. It was voted upon this morning. The sigil would rather she stay in the Natttie world and fend for herself. But the majority of us believe she'd be an asset to our kind."

I glanced at my father again who was staring back at me, a muscle working in his jaw.

"Brighton assures us she'll be ready by the time the new year starts. That being said, we would like a watch on her," Sangrey's deep voice commanded my attention back on him. "And we'd like to see the girl trained once her sanity comes back to her. I can't imagine her journey has been an easy one. If she is truly what we believe her to be, we want her trained and inducted into Conexus."

"No," I shot back angrily. "She will *not* join Conexus."

"And why is that, General?" Sir Broderick stared me down, the other members of the Order all focused on me.

I knew they wanted me to admit she was the Mancer and I was the Reever. And if what my father said was true, I couldn't let whoever the snake was have *that* information. "Your chapter takes in the rarest of gifts. Your second in command is a stitcher. Your third in command can shift into incredible things that no other shifter can. Even Amara is one of the strongest, most cunning of wolves. So tell me, why would you *not* want a trophy like a whisperer in your group?"

"Because. I don't accept anyone into my chapter who demonstrates mental illness," I seethed out, lying. "It would be unwise to do so."

"So you agree she's unstable?" Sir Mathis raised an eyebrow at me.

"I agree she's under duress and needs guidance. It would take a lot to get the girl in the position to join our ranks."

"You do realize that a whisperer hasn't been around for centuries, correct?" Sir Broderick broke in. "And you do realize that this is a *huge* deal? We *need* this kind of member in Conexus. We need her on our side, unwavering in her loyalty. We'd like to see her trained and within the ranks of the elite by winter. Students at Dementon train well past what a Nattie does. She'll be a student at Dementon for at least two more years. We educate well past what the Nattie schools do."

"I do not wish to have a whisperer in my ranks," I ground out.

"Why, General?" Sir LaCroix asked with a raised eyebrow.

"Because," I breathed out evenly, my father's words from our last visit echoing in my mind. "They are an abomination to our kind. An anomaly that needn't receive special treatment. I will *not* employ one."

"Dude, what the hell," Damien muttered.

"Mr. Wick, do you have something to say in regard to what your esteemed leader has declared?" Sir Sangrey leveled his gaze on Damien.

*"It's not what you think. They want to test her to see if she's the Mancer. We can't let that happen,"* I declared, using my telepathy on Damien.

"I have to agree with my general. I don't want to see a whisperer in our ranks. It's bad enough that we encounter the lost ones. To have a member *plagued* by them would only drive us nuts. We can barely stand hunting them. To have them lurking about whenever we go out would be a distraction and create more work for us. We need our wits about us. A whisperer would only drag us down," Damien's voice boomed out.

"Amara, thoughts? It seems your general thought highly enough of you to bring you. Care to weigh in?" Sir Mathis raised his eyebrow at her.

"I don't want a whisperer in our ranks either," she sniffed. "But not *only* for the reasons my general and Damien have mentioned. I feel as if her being there will cause conflict in mine and the general's already struggling relationship."

"Amara," I warned softly.

She continued to speak, ignoring me, "We cannot make our relationship work if *he's* constantly worried about her. I'd like to see her assigned to work with our second in command, Eric Craft. *He* can train her. Maybe under his guidance, the girl will gain some semblance of normality. For one thing, we don't even know if she can handle the fights and hunts we go on. I mean, she can *see* the dead.

176

What strengths could she possibly bring to the table other than that? I think we need to weigh everything properly before extending a welcome letter to her. After some time with Eric, then perhaps we can reconsider her joining us. Perhaps even as early as the spring since winter doesn't seem to be to my general's liking."

"I see," Sir Sangrey said, sitting back in his seat.

"It seems Amara has her head about her." Sir Mathis nodded. Sir LaCroix beamed proudly at his daughter. "She's made some very valid points.

"I like this idea. I'd like to see how she progresses as well without the pressure of what being in Conexus could mean for her. Perhaps Amara is correct. We do not know what the girl is even capable of. *You will make a fine queen one day.*" Sir Sangrey nodded slowly. *What was his deal? Whose side was he on?*

Amara beamed wider at the compliment.

"So, that's settled. Are we done?" I snapped.

"No." Sir Broderick shook his head. "We have many other items on our list tonight. I suggest you get comfortable."

"We have intel that the Cipher is gathering forces in the southern regions. There are increasing numbers of haunts on the rise. Wraiths have been spotted as far north as your ghost whisperer's home. The carrion have been attacking, seemingly without cause other than by orders of the Cipher. New vampires are being created—"

"What?" I asked, surprised at the news.

"Ah, yes." Sir Mathis nodded. "It's true, General. Our eastern Conexus chapter took out a nest of over twenty fledglings. It's against Order law to create a new vampire. Vampires are to be born, not created, unless otherwise specified or declared by the Order. Natties have no business coming into our world so easily."

"I wouldn't call *that* easy," Damien argued. "Vampire venom is among some of the most painful poisons in the known world to experience. Not all who are bitten, survive."

"Nor would I," Sir Broderick agreed. "However, that's what's been happening. We're assuming the Cipher is involved. The Overlord Aviram has been known to go to extreme measures with his fights.

He's proven once again his disregard for our way of life. He *must* be dealt with."

"We've been trying to deal with him," I replied. "He leads the Cipher. How do you want us to deal with him? He cannot be found. He's well-hidden and protected. His numbers vastly outweigh our own. The Conexus would have to work around the clock to keep up with him."

"And are you *not* concerned," my father inquired, finally speaking up. "Surely, as the future of our world, you should be."

"I didn't say I wasn't. I only said that he has far more numbers than we do. What do you expect us to do? We hunt, we fight, we kill. We bring members of the Cipher here to you for questioning—"

"Ah, which brings us to another point before I forget," Sir Sangrey interrupted. "We have a task for you! An honor really."

"What's that?" I asked, my mouth going dry. The members of the Order began whispering to one another, their heads bobbing as they spoke.

"I don't think we're going to like this," Damien murmured.

"Me either," I replied. Even Amara stiffened beside me.

"General, we're going to bestow the honor of interrogation to you and your two ranking officers. We've brought in some of the best in our Conexus chapters. We'd like you to head it up for us. You have an impressive track record with getting information out of our enemies. We voted, and you won by unanimous vote. We're calling the group F.I.R.E. It's something new we're trying." Sir Broderick beamed widely at us.

"What's it mean?" I asked wearily, looking at Damien since he'd be a part of it with me.

"It stands for the Federation of Interrogation, Reformation, and Extermination. You'd come here to interrogate those captured. You'd dole out the punishments and exterminate as needed," Sir Sangrey explained, his eyes focused on me.

"What do you mean, *exterminate*?" I demanded. "*Who* would we be exterminating?"

"Anyone you're told to," Sir Sangrey answered darkly.

"Anyone?" Damien asked. "I don't like being told to kill people. What if they're innocent?"

"Then you'd best hope you interrogate properly or you'll have a lot of blood on your hands," Sir Mathis replied with a shrug.

"Do we get a choice in joining or is this like the Conexus?" I growled, growing angry with where the Order was heading. They were power hungry. It was unlike them to act this way. They'd always been fair for the most part. But this didn't seem fair or right.

"No. It's another honor. Congratulations!" Sir Mathis beamed like he'd done us a favor.

"This is bullshit," I snapped.

"Watch your tone, General!" my father bellowed. I ground my teeth together angrily but said nothing.

They droned on and on for hours about recent attacks, leads, what other chapters had brought them in regard to prisoners. My eyes grew heavier with each passing minute. When I was ready to fall asleep, they finally said something that made me jolt.

"You'll begin tonight," Sir Broderick declared.

"I'm sorry, *what*?" I asked, frowning.

"General, there are prisoners housed in the dungeons. They will be brought to the Citadel for questioning. You and Mr. Wick will do what you must to get information out of them."

"And if they won't speak?" I demanded, feeling sick to my stomach.

"Then F.I.R.E. If you catch my meaning."

# CHAPTER 37

$\mathcal{W}$e left the Circle to escort Amara back to the portal.

"Good luck," she murmured, turning to me.

"You really pissed me off tonight," I growled, grabbing her roughly by the arm. Damien took a step away to give us space. "*Why* would you do that?"

"Because you're *not* thinking clearly," she snapped, jerking her arm out of my grasp. "This girl has cast a spell on you! You and I used to lie for hours just talking to one another. The moment she came into the picture, it all ended! *She's* the reason we aren't together!"

"We *never* lay for hours talking," I said softly. "I always got up and left as soon as… we were done. You're trying to make me into something I'll never be, Amara. Why can't you just let me go?"

"I love you," she sniffed. "And I know that after all this blows over, you'll love me too. I just have to have hope."

"Please just stop." I closed my eyes and breathed out. "I don't want *anyone*, Amara. Not you. Not E-Everly." I stumbled on her name, my mouth knowing I was lying. My heart too. "No one. I'm better off alone. I'm not boyfriend material. And I'm certainly not marriage material."

"You are," she said passionately. "If you'd just let yourself go, you'd see that! You'd see how good we are together! How good we could be!"

"I'm probably going to go kill someone tonight," I murmured as I looked down at her. "This isn't a good conversation for me to have right now, Mara. Just go home. Rest. OK?"

"OK," she said, her voice soft. I looked at her in surprise. *She wasn't arguing with me.* That was short-lived. "Will you kiss me before I go?"

"Amara," I sighed, shaking my head, backing away.

"Please!" She grabbed my hands. "Please."

"You promise you won't do this again?" I asked.

"I promise."

I ground my teeth before leaning down and pressing my mouth to hers. I didn't put much effort into it. But she did. Her lips parted as she let out a soft moan into my mouth, her tongue sliding against mine. I couldn't figure out why she continued to torture herself this way or why I gave her the means to.

"For two people who aren't seeing one another, you look awfully cozy," my father commented. I quickly yanked away from Amara who wore a small smirk on her face. She'd done that on purpose. Damien shook his head at me.

"She was just leaving," I snarled, glaring at Amara. She had the decency to blush.

"Shadow—" she started but I shook my head at her angrily, not wanting to hear anything she had to say. She snapped her mouth closed and stepped into the portal, disappearing from view.

"I don't know why you fight it. You clearly like one another," my father mused. I only glared at him. "I was only coming to find you. I was worried you may have skipped out."

"I don't *skip* out on my duties." I made to push past him, but he caught my arm.

"*This* is important, Son. Your duties are about to get harder. We need answers, and you're the kind of man who can get them. We're counting on you. If everything I said to you earlier was true, we need this more than ever. We need to know where to find Aviram. Our next step is to interrogate his nephew."

"You can't bring innocent people in and torture them," I growled, ripping my arm from his grasp roughly. "Nevron Blackburn has done *nothing* wrong."

"He's the overlord's nephew. Surely he knows his whereabouts."

"The guy is a douche, but he isn't in league with his uncle," I snapped. "He's more concerned with getting chicks into bed with him, his hair, and what blood type he'll have for dinner."

"I want you to keep an eye on him," my father stated firmly. "If anything suspicious happens—"

"Then I'll do what I must," I barked at him. "Now let's get this over with. I have better things to be doing."

"I'm sure you do," my father murmured knowingly. I ignored him. I had to make sure Everly was OK. This was the first time none of us would be available for her.

# CHAPTER 38

"I don't know anything!" the vampire screamed at us, his eyes wild. "I'm not a part of the Cipher!"

"Our intel suggests otherwise," I replied grimly, picking up a pair of pliers and turning them over in my hands. The vamp eyed them wearily, his brows beading with sweat.

"I swear to you, I know nothing. I was just in the wrong place at the wrong time. I'll even show you through Mesmire!"

"I'm not interested in your vampire mind tricks," I sighed tiredly. He was our sixth vampire of the night to interrogate. So far, none had yielded results.

"They *aren't* mind tricks! You're a general in the Conexus. I know how powerful you are. You can look and see for yourself! Why won't you?" The vampire wept, his head hanging forward. "You're one of the most powerful creatures in our world, and yet you're in here, torturing innocent Specials! Where are your morals?"

"It's been a long night," Damien spoke up tiredly as I rubbed my chest, frowning. My connection to Everly was warning me. I had to get out of there.

"Kill him," I declared, feeling woozy. One less vamp in the world was fine by me.

"*What?*" Both the vamp and Damien asked, surprised.

"You heard me. Kill him. Make him an example. I have more pressing matters to get to," I snapped.

"Gen, you can't be serious! He's done nothing wrong that I can see," Damien argued, paling. "Don't let your connection rule your mind."

I leaned weakly against the wall, sweat dotting my brow. I looked up at the vamp in front of me. He looked terrified. I stormed toward him, my feet unsteady. I went down to him abruptly and gazed into his eyes.

"Show me," I demanded. The vamp nodded weakly, his body shaking. A moment later I was seeing into his mind with his Mesmire. He was a former student at Dementon. He'd spent the last week in his home, heartsick over his vamp girlfriend leaving him for a lock. Last night he'd gone out to a vamp bar. Wrong place at the wrong time. I pulled away from him in disgust.

"Release him. He's innocent," I snarled.

"Come on, man." Damien undid his silver chains and hauled him to his feet. "Run. Fast. Before Gen changes his mind."

The vamp didn't need to be told twice. He rushed out as soon as Damien tossed him out the door declaring his freedom.

"You OK?" Damien asked.

"Something's wrong with her," I mumbled, feeling dizzy.

"She can do this tonight. Have faith in her," Damien said softly. "Let's just finish this so we can leave. OK?"

"OK," I murmured.

The next prisoner was brought in. We spent the night going through every single one of them. By the end of it, I'd been attacked twice and had beaten my attackers to barely breathing. Damien had to yank me off them. The awful feelings coming from my connection to Everly were fueling my fire. I was weak and barely standing by the end of it.

"What did you find out?" Sangrey asked, coming into the room as I wiped a vamp's blood from my face and hands.

"That I don't want to do this shit," I muttered, tossing the rag aside.

"No one wants to," Sangrey scoffed. "But in times of war, we have to do things we don't want to do."

"No, *you* don't have to do shit," I snarled. "*We* do. Honor my ass! This is bullshit and you know it, Sangrey! What's really going on here? These prisoners were only guilty of minor infractions."

"You don't catch a fish every time you go fishing." Sangrey smirked at me. "You know that, General. These creatures will go home tonight spreading the word of our power. Of *your* power."

"That's what this was about?" I demanded. "Inciting fear?"

"Fear is a useful tool. You of all people know that." Sangrey gave me a tight smile. "Now, they know what we're willing to do. Word will travel fast."

"I didn't do this to be a damn bully to the innocent!"

"You have to see the greater good in it."

"There is *no* good in destroying innocent people," I hissed at him. Damien touched me lightly on the arm, a signal for me to calm myself.

"You just need to look past the innocent and see the wicked that stands behind them," Sangrey said darkly.

"I'm done. I'm going home," I snapped.

"Mr. Wick, would you excuse us? I'd like a word with my nephew," Sangrey said, his eyes focused on me.

"I'm not in the mood—" I started. Sangrey's eyes slid to Damien who cast me a quick look before exiting.

"I *know* that you still see the girl. And I know you lied to the Order," Sangrey's voice held no judgement. I glared at him.

"Are you going to do anything about it?" I asked.

"No." He shook his head. "I trust you know what you're doing." My shoulders slumped as I relaxed at his words. "You're upset because of her. Your connection has been going wild all night, hasn't it?"

"Yes," I murmured.

"Then by all means, go to her. You're free for now. I'm sure we'll be calling on you again soon. Oh, and give Mr. Craft my regards. That was indeed a big stitch."

I swallowed hard and backed away. My uncle always had eyes in all corners of the world. I don't know why I was surprised he knew about Eric. I nodded silently to him and left quickly.

"How'd it go?" Damien asked as I met him at the portal.

"I just need to make sure Everly is OK," I murmured, stepping into the portal.

# CHAPTER 39

"She's fine," Damien proclaimed, coming into Eric's room later that morning. I'd been too weak to go to her after my night filled with torturing people. Damien said he'd go and report back. "She's just her usual depressed self."

"Sounds about right." Eric yawned. I'd just finished telling him about our night and how he was now a member F.I.R.E. He hadn't seemed happy about it, but he wasn't the only one feeling angry.

"What's the verdict?" Damien asked, sitting down on the edge of Eric's bed.

"About what?" Eric asked.

"Everly. You going to take care of her or what?" Damien pressed.

"No." Eric shook his head, his eyes not meeting mine. I didn't say anything. I wasn't going to push it. I knew he'd give in eventually. He usually did.

"You're nuts," Damien snorted. "That girl is gorgeous. Are you worried you won't be able to keep your hands off her tight little body?"

Eric flushed, and I let out a low growl.

"That's it, isn't it?" Damien's eyes lit up. "You're worried about getting too close to her!"

"I am *not*." He shook his head quickly.

"Yes, you are! You don't have to sleep with her. *Damn*. Calm down. You're just going to be friends with her! I don't understand why you're making this into such a big deal." Damien looked at him in disbelief.

"I'm making it a big deal because it's a lie! I don't lie to people! In fact, I hate it and don't tolerate it. What am I supposed to tell her when it's over? 'Hey, this was great, but this wasn't a real friendship. I'm out.' No. I won't be a part of it. If I'm her friend, it's because there's no other motive than I simply think she's cool and we click. Anything past that violates my morals."

"Your morals," Damien snorted. "You banged that chick from that vamp bar in Detroit behind a dumpster in the alley while me and Shadow—" He gestured between me and him. "—took out her Cipher brother. Where were your morals then?"

Eric's face darkened, and he looked down wordlessly, frustration on his face. There was a moment of silence before he finally spoke, "What if something happens between us? I'm not saying it *will*, but what if?" He looked at me with wide eyes. "I get the reason for this. I do. It's just, the what ifs are driving me nuts. I can't do that to you, man..." his voice trailed off, his face reddening.

"I know," I managed to say, my guts twisting at the realness of his words. He was right. The what ifs *were* potential problems. I'd already thought about them and pushed them away, telling myself that Eric was trustworthy. And I still believed that.

"Screw it. I'll do it," Damien stated.

"What?" I frowned.

"I said I'll do it. She won't get much conversation or whatever it is chicks like, but I'll do my best to keep her occupied. I'll teach her how to headlock someone. And if she falls for me, then I won't say anything to you about what we do. In fact, I'll be a gentleman and tell her I'm saving myself for marriage."

"No." Eric let out a big sigh. "I'll do it."

"You will?" I asked. My mouth felt like I was sucking on a cotton ball.

"Yeah. Just don't get pissed at me for trying to hang out with her. If things go south, you can't get all crazy jealous and try to kill me because this was *your* idea."

"Craft, you act like she's going to jump your bones. She's just a lost girl looking for help. You're just going to be friends. Stop weighing every freaking scenario. If things start to go there, then just come to Shadow and tell him." Damien rolled his eyes.

"I just don't like surprises," he muttered. "And I suck at trying to be friends with girls. I weird them out because of my mind stuff."

"We'll help you." Damien grinned. "Right, Shadow?"

"Right," I answered tightly.

"This is so messed up," Eric grumbled, closing his eyes and sinking back onto his pillows tiredly. "I'm going to have to be a chick's best friend. Should I buy her nail polish or something? I don't even know what girls do for fun."

"You'll be training her so that should be easy for you." I shrugged. "Most of your time will be spent in the gym. I'm sure she's going to need a lot of help with it. Just offer to work with her on her skills and abilities. Show her how to do a spinning back kick. I'm sure that's not something she knows how to do."

"That might not be so bad." He relaxed a bit, closing his eyes. "But what if she asks me about *you*, Shadow? She knows you're a Special, or at least she will. What do I do then?"

"Then be me," I said softly.

"What?" Eric opened his eyes and peered at me.

"Confess that you're me. That you're Shadow. Then you'll be a shoo in for her," I replied sadly.

"No. Way." Eric shook his head, his blond hair falling in his eyes. "No way. Hell no."

"If you have to, do it," I returned morosely. "Anything to keep her focused on you."

"She'll hate us both if she ever finds out!" Eric argued.

"She'll hate us either way. Maybe it's better that way." I hung my head, hating that I was going to go ahead with this plan knowing damn well that the *what ifs* were very real. Eric had *saved* her. He was a hero in her eyes. A hero who was real, tangible, and easily obtainable.

And I'd always be a secret.

# CHAPTER 40

*D*amien set out again the next night to watch over Everly. I stayed with Eric, feeling uncomfortable.

"I don't want our friendship to get ruined over this," Eric commented with a sigh as we lounged on the couch in the commons. He was finally getting enough strength to move around.

"It won't," I answered firmly. "You don't have to get romantic with her, Eric. Just be a good friend. Shit talk about the guys. Make her hate them all." I chuckled softly.

"I can do that." Eric nodded.

"If that doesn't work, then we can enact Plan B—Damien. How does that sound?"

"Like a huge weight has been lifted off my shoulders."

We laughed and talked throughout the evening, for once our lives feeling normal again, or as normal as our lives could seem considering who we were. Sloane and Amanda even joined us. When Damien burst through the door, his face red, we were hooting loudly as Sloane told the story of how she hit him in the face with an empty milk carton a few nights ago.

"What's wrong?" I asked, getting to my feet. I hadn't felt anything wrong with Everly.

"That douche has her at his place. What do you want me to do, man? We didn't go over that shit! I know how to deal with the lost ones, wraiths, Cipher, whatever. Throw me in with a Nattie teenager who wants to get off with a girl he doesn't belong with and the only thing I know how to do is hit."

"Slow down. What's going on?" I was pulling my cloak on as he talked.

"She's wasted. High. Drunk. I don't know. Brighton has her on a crap ton of Nattie meds. She was feeling particularly morose tonight. I figured she'd sleep it off. Instead, she went straight to that douche Dylan and planted her mouth on his. He took her away. I slipped into the backseat with them. He was feeling her up, and he took her to his house. I can only imagine what's going on right now. If you want to save her, now would be a really good time," Damien finished up breathlessly, his eyes bright.

"Show me where he lives," I growled. We melded quickly. I followed him to a large home in the ritzy part of a neighborhood.

"She's in there with him. Upstairs. Third door on the left. Want me to go with you?"

"No, stand guard out here," I said, my voice soft and dangerous. My hands shook as I tried to regain control of myself. I tried to run different scenarios through my mind, but I knew the only one that would greet me, and I needed to prepare for it.

Slowly, I walked up his stairs and paused outside his bedroom door, listening.

"Ever, baby, come on. Relax," Dylan's voice cooed. My body went rigid, all my anger coming to the surface. He was *touching* her. I let out a deep growl, knowing I was going to lose myself to my anger in mere moments. Maybe I should've had Damien come with me. I winced as the distant sound of the lost ones surrounded me, their voices frantic.

"Dylan, stop. Please," Everly's voice pleaded. *That was it. No one touched her. No one!* I swept into the room and let my shadow-self shimmer into view at the foot of his bed. She was beneath him, her shirt drawn up, his body tangled over hers. His hands were in places on her body that made me see red.

I didn't hesitate as my anger grew. The dead shouted in the distance. They were terrified of me. *Good*. They should be. I pushed my will for them to disappear and was greeted by their silence as they faded away.

Reaching forward, I plucked Dylan off her as if he weighed nothing. Members of Conexus were strong—stupid strong when in shade form. He flailed in my hands before I threw him across the room. He landed with a thud against the wall, and I stalked purposefully to him. His eyes were wild as he peered through the dim light to figure out what had happened to him. He couldn't see me. One of my perks of being Conexus.

"No!" Everly screamed, stumbling as she tried to untangle herself from his bedsheets. "No. Don't hurt him!"

I ignored her and leaned down to wrap my fingers around Dylan's neck. I'd been waiting for that moment for a long time. He choked and sputtered in protest, his eyes wild as he tried to claw at me.

"Stop! Please, stop!" Everly sobbed. Her hand reached out for me and touched my shoulder. I loosened my grip on Dylan's neck and stared at her. She was drunk. Her eyes were wild, her hair a mess. Where her shirt was pulled up, the soft skin of her abdomen was exposed. She trembled as she touched me, her lower lip shaking as she silently pleaded with me.

She didn't understand. This guy didn't care about her. He wanted what every other guy who looked at her wanted. And she wasn't in her right mind to decide this. He *knew* that, and he still took advantage of her!

He had to pay. I came to that decision easily and tightened my hold on his neck. Lifting him into the air, I let his feet dangle just off the ground. He flailed and tried to claw at me, but he couldn't hurt what he couldn't see. From the corner of my eye, I caught Everly sobbing. My heart hurt. I wouldn't kill him. I'd just leave him with a warning.

"She's *mine*. She belongs to me and *only* me. I'm the only one who will touch her. I am the only one she'll ever love. You are *nothing* to her. You will never be anything to her. Tell her to leave. Tell her you don't want her here. Do you understand?"

"I-I understand," he managed to choke out, his eyes darting to Everly and back again. I released him, and he slid to the floor in a crumpled heap.

"Dylan!" Everly rushed to him but he backed away as she reached for him.

"Go away, Ever." He shrank away from her.

"Wh-why? Let me help you!" She tried again, but he pushed her away.

"You need to go. Now. Leave, Ever! I don't want you here," Dylan's voice was as firm as he was insistent.

"I-I'm sorry," she whispered, grabbing her jacket off the floor. She tugged it on and glared at me like I was the bad guy. But I'd only done what I'd promised. I did my job. I protected her. That meant from guys like Dylan.

But the way she looked at me made my heart clench. She backed away, stumbling out the door, getting as far from me as she could get.

# CHAPTER 41

"*I figured you'd need help,*" Eric's voice called out to me in my head.

"*How'd you know where to find me?*" I asked, watching as Dylan struggled to his feet after lying in the same spot for fifteen minutes.

"*Damien. He thought you might go nuts, so he came and got me.*" Eric looked interestedly at Dylan who seemed confused as he stumbled around, rubbing his head.

"*I messed up,*" I said, looking from Dylan to Eric.

"*I figured,*" Eric's voice sounded like he was smiling. "*Clean up, aisle seven?*"

"*Yeah,*" I muttered.

"*I can make him forget. Or alter what he thought happened.*"

"*Change the memory. If you can. I know you're tired,*" I replied.

"*I'm fine,*" Eric said, stepping toward Dylan. He placed his hands on either side of Dylan's head in the same manner as Brandon did when he healed. A dazed look fell over Dylan's face, but he didn't struggle. Eric's hands glowed blue like they did when he stitched. He closed his eyes, and Dylan's face went slack. A moment later, Eric released him and backed away.

"Shit," Dylan sighed, sitting on his bed and rubbing his eyes. He withdrew his phone and dialed a number. A frown turned his lips down. He let out a frustrated sigh and hung the phone up. Finally, he got to his feet and went downstairs. A moment later, his front door closed, and his car rumbled.

"What did you *do?*" I asked.

"I made him think they were making out, and she got mad and stormed out. I erased you and everything from his mind. Fixed."

"Thanks," I said, nodding. "I was going to kill him."

"Killing innocent Natties is frowned upon, even for members of Conexus," Eric teased. I grinned at him and looked to the board Dylan had on his wall. Photos of his friends covered it. My eyes narrowed in on Everly's face. She was wearing a pretty purple sundress, her hair cascading around her. It was wavy, a look I'd never seen on her before. She was smiling shyly at the camera, her green eyes sparkling. She was breathtaking. I reached out and grabbed the photo off the board.

"Keepsake?" Eric asked mildly.

"Yeah," I mumbled, stuffing it in my pocket. I'd add it to the other photo of her I had that I'd taken the first night I'd been pulled back to her.

"We should probably go find her," Eric commented as we went downstairs and outside to where Damien was waiting.

"No need," I grabbed at my chest, the mark on my wrist burning. "I'll find her easily enough."

# CHAPTER 42

"What the hell did she do?" I shouted, sweeping into the liquor store to find her on her back, foaming vomit dripping from her mouth. The store clerk was on his knees beside her, talking rapidly into the phone. I'd shimmered to invisibility before arriving and put my hands on her chest. She was *so* drunk.

Pain stabbed in my chest, stealing my breath. She'd tried drinking herself to death. The thought sickened me, and I blamed myself for her lying there. I put all my energy into taking it from her. As the transfer started, I felt woozy. When it was complete, I sank back. Eric and Damien caught me before I fell completely backward.

The ambulance arrived, and she was loaded into the back. I could barely see straight.

"Shit. You're wasted now," Damien said, trying to keep me upright as I stumbled all over.

"This would be comical if it wasn't so serious," Eric added, grunting as he caught me again before I fell.

"I feel… not good," I mumbled, my words slurred, my eyes heavy. "Is she OK?" I swayed forward, and the guys snagged me before I hit the ground.

"She'll be OK. She just needs to sleep it off," Damien grumbled, pulling me back upright. "Why don't you heal yourself, so we don't have to carry your ass back?"

"Cannnn't," I slurred. "Can't heal when it'sssss from her. Takes time. And we can't heal being drunk any-anyway," I hiccuped, my vision swimming. "I think I'm going to be sick."

No sooner were the words out of my mouth than I was throwing up. Eric let out a yelp as he dodged out of the way. Thank God the guys had managed to get me outside and to a dark corner of the lot. I couldn't maintain my shadow. I was now a full blown teenage guy heaving my guts out in a bush wearing all black, a cloak, and a whole lot of weapons.

"Remember that time we all got trashed when we took out that forsaken last year?" Damien asked, referring to the vamp who'd gone bloodlust.

"Yeah, that was good stuff," Eric spoke loudly over the sound of my heaving.

"Shadow got so wasted that night. He ended up making out with both Amara *and* that Nattie he met at the mall. Too bad he didn't do it together with them." Damien chuckled.

"I'm dying." I fell backward. "This is so much worse than that night."

"Isn't love grand?" Damien grinned, looming over me as I stared up to him. I couldn't focus. There were three of him.

"We should get him home." Eric's head came into view, and I blinked and groaned. They shared a laugh before getting me to my feet.

"Hold on, brother. This probably won't feel good," Eric said, his arm around me and Damien on my other side. There was a pulling in my guts, the feeling that always accompanied being melded by someone else.

I wasn't able to stand anymore as Eric and Damien hauled me into the commons.

"What the hell happened to him now?" Brandon asked.

"Is he *drunk*?" Sloane's voice called out.

"Dude, you guys went and partied without us?" Adam complained.

"Shut up and help us. He's a flopper," Damien grunted. I was lifted into the air by Brandon, Damien, Eric, and Adam and dropped unceremoniously on the couch.

"Better get a bucket, Sloane. Pretty sure he's going to barf again," Damien muttered. A moment later there was a bucket beside my head. Sloane thrust a bottle of water into my hands.

"Drink. You'll hate yourself in the morning if you don't."

"I hate mysssself right now," I slurred, taking a drink of the water. Immediately, I leaned over and heaved into the bucket again.

"What the hell did you guys do to him?" Brandon whistled.

"He, uh, drank too much," Eric added delicately. I knew they wouldn't tell them what I'd really done. Sure, it seemed funny for me to be wasted out of my mind, but if they knew I'd done it to save Everly, there would be a different attitude among them. There hadn't even been a moment's hesitation when it came to saving her. I knew my father wanted whatever happened, to happen. I just couldn't do it. She was mine to keep safe.

"Are we having a party?" Jared asked as he came into the room with Amara and Amanda.

"Yeah, you missed it," Damien said. "Gen was dancing without his shirt a minute ago."

I gave him the finger as I continued to puke in the bucket.

"Are you kidding me? Why the hell did you guys let him drink so much?" Amara demanded, coming to sit beside me. Moaning, I fell back, my head spinning. The water was pressed to my lips again, and I sloshed it around in my mouth before spitting it into the bucket. I took another drink, this one greedily. It felt good to fill my stomach.

I said a silent prayer that Everly didn't ever drink that much again.

## CHAPTER 43

"How you feeling, man?" Eric greeted me the next morning. With a groan, I rubbed my eyes. I was still on the couch. The bucket was gone. I took the bottle of water that Eric offered and sucked it down quickly, my head feeling like it was close to bursting.

"Shit," I mumbled, wiping my eyes. "That's rough."

"If it helps, she's not feeling much better," Eric added. "I went and checked on her. Headmaster Brighton left Ceres there to guard her door."

"Yeah, like *that* won't terrify her. She'll think Ceres is one of *them*."

"Brighton is attending to her. He told me to tell you that this is it. The push we needed to get her here. Her mom signed the papers this morning."

"What?" I sat up straighter and focused my eyes on him.

"Yep. She's being transported right now to Rolling Thunder Psychiatric Facility. Both Brighton and Damien are with her right now. She's out cold, but when she wakes up, she'll be within the facility walls. She's almost here. In just a week she'll be safe, man."

I didn't know what to say. Instead, I brushed at my eyes, removing the moisture and feeling like a total wuss. But she was coming. We'd

203

done it. Everly was going to be at Dementon soon. I was beside myself with happiness.

"Tell me how you really feel." Eric chuckled, slapping me on the back. I let out a soft laugh and sniffled.

"I'm just so relieved." I breathed out.

"Well, she was pretty bad off. Brighton said he had to booty dart her to get her to calm down. He put her under because she was going nuts."

"What do you mean?" I asked, my heart racing for entirely new reasons.

"I guess she told her mom she was trying to kill herself," Eric winced. "Brighton is going to do one final round of questioning with her. He wants you to be there. Think you can handle it?"

"Yeah." I nodded, getting to my feet. I swayed for a moment before getting right. I blinked a few times then gave Eric a reassuring smile. "I'm going to grab a shower."

"Take your time. Brighton said it would be at least an hour before they got there since they were traveling the Nattie way in an ambulance. Plus, at least another hour before she'd probably wake up."

That was a decent amount of time to get rehydrated and grab something to eat. I rushed to my bathroom and quickly showered and dressed, tugging my silver hair into a knot and donning my all black attire. When I went downstairs I found Eric and Sloane eating in the kitchen.

"Hey," Sloane greeted me.

"Hey." I smiled at her.

"Wow. You look happy!" she commented, pushing a turkey sandwich at me.

"I am." I grinned again.

"Guess you need to get shitfaced more often." She handed me a glass of water as Eric cast me a sidelong look.

"Yeah, I don't think I want to do that again anytime soon," I muttered, digging into my sandwich. I felt at ease knowing Everly would soon be here with me. Even if she wasn't *with* me, she'd be near enough, and she'd be safe within the walls of Dementon. Nothing would dare come *here* to touch her.

"You coming with me?" I asked Eric.

"No." He looked amused. "Actually, I think I'm going to chill here. I feel like a tremendous weight has been lifted off my shoulders. So, I sort of want to enjoy it for a day or two."

"I hear you." I squeezed his shoulder. I went out the door and melded, skipping through the shadows like I didn't have a care in the world. Even though Everly had finally broken, we could fix her now. We could keep her safe.

And maybe I'd finally get to have a real conversation with her once she got here.

# CHAPTER 44

Frowning, I entered the basement of Rolling Thunder. In the short amount of time it had taken for me to meld there, something had changed. Everly was awake. And she was frightened. Because of our connection, I knew where she was being kept. I rushed down the hallway, the fluorescent lights buzzing overhead.

When I appeared in the room, it was to find two large vamp orderlies wrestling with her. She was a wild animal, tearing at them, her nails scratching at whatever she could reach. She bit one ferociously. The vamp immediately lashed out and punched her in the face. My form shimmered before I became myself again, dressed all in black, my hood pulled low over my head. I growled as Everly's head snapped to the side, her eyes dazed, her body limp.

When I rushed forward they dropped Everly to the ground. They knew who I was and what I was capable of. I flung the vamp orderlies aside as if they were nothing at all.

"Help," she called out as I scooped her small body up off the floor. Headmaster Brighton began reprimanding the men. That was only the beginning of what was going to happen to them once Everly was resting comfortably.

"Please. Let me die," her voice was hoarse, her eyes fluttering.

"Where's the fun in that?" I murmured as her eyes finally closed, her body relaxing against my chest. I breathed out deeply in relief as I held her. She was here. In my arms. Where she belonged.

Cradling her close, I stalked out of the room. Brighton caught up to me at the end of the hallway.

"They will be dealt with," he said evenly as I held Everly.

"I'll see to it," I said darkly. Brighton let out a sigh but didn't argue.

"I'll show you to her room," he said as we got into the elevator. We didn't talk as we rode to the fourth floor. When we got there, I followed him out of the elevator to a room down the hall. He opened the door and gestured for me to enter. I did so and laid Everly onto her small bed.

"Everything will get better now, Everly," I murmured in her ear. She didn't respond to me.

"She'll be out for a few hours," Headmaster Brighton said from the doorway of the small room. I nodded tightly as I pushed her damp hair away from her face.

"Give us a moment, please," I said. The door closed signaling him leaving. I reached down and took Everly's hand in mine and gave it a squeeze. If she happened to wake in that moment, she'd see me—the *real* me, the guy with the silver hair and aquamarine eyes. She'd see my tall, muscular stature. She'd finally meet *me*. The thought had my heart thrashing in my chest. I wasn't ready for that. It wasn't time for that. She needed to get comfortable with Dementon. With herself. I couldn't add to it just yet. But eventually we'd get to meet.

"I've been waiting forever for you," I whispered, planting a tender kiss on her temple as she slumbered. "I can wait a little longer. I promise everything will work out, Everly. Even if we can't be together because of what we are. I swear I'll continue to protect you. You're mine. Forever."

## CHAPTER 45

*I* went back home feeling hopeful after I spent a good half an hour roughing up Brighton's vamp orderlies. I knew they wouldn't forget me anytime soon.

"You're back early," Damien commented.

"Yeah, I'm surprised I didn't see you at the facility," I said, hanging my cloak on the rack by the door.

"I was so hungry I thought I was going to die." He stuffed a large bite of pizza into his mouth. Eric chuckled from the chair he sat in. "Figured you had it. I thought she'd still be out anyway. She was right?"

"She was awake for a bit. But yeah, she was out when I left." When I told them about what happened with the orderlies. Eric shook his head angrily.

"I *hate* those guys. Brighton insists he needs them. Just because they're vamps and a little stronger than the rest of the Specials doesn't mean he should employ them. Some of them are a little touched in the head if you want my opinion."

"I agree," Damien said, swallowing. "I almost punched one in the face earlier. He shoved Everly into her bed so hard I was afraid she was going to go *through* the mattress."

I shook my head, glad I'd thrown them around like rag dolls.

"I was thinking we should celebrate." Damien pulled out a bottle of tarish, and I chuckled.

"I don't think I can." I laughed even louder as he waggled his brows at me.

"Come on, man. She's coming. In just a week, that beautiful girl is going to be walking our campus. No more late-night runs. No more worrying. No more anything. She'll be *here*. Safe. If that ain't a reason to celebrate, then I don't know what is."

"You're right." I grinned widely. "Pour me a drink, brother."

"Atta boy!" Damien proclaimed, opening the bottle while Eric grabbed glasses.

"Are you guys breaking Dementon rules by drinking on campus?" Sloane called out.

"Yep" Damien smirked up at her.

"Just checking. I'll put the wards up on the doors." She hurried to the door and started muttering quickly. Her hands lit with a dull purple glow. She took a step back and smirked at the door. "That ought to do the trick!"

"Not that it matters considering we're the ones in charge of policing this sort of thing on campus." Eric laughed loudly. I joined in when Sloane looked indignant.

"Get over here and celebrate with us," Damien called out to her. She bounced over and took the glass he offered her.

"What are we celebrating?"

"Everly," I said softly, smiling. Sloane's grin grew wider, and she clinked her glass against mine.

"About damn time!" she said loudly.

"About damn time," I agreed gently, taking a drink from my glass, the smile not leaving my lips.

# CHAPTER 46

*J* awoke sometime before dawn with that familiar, god-awful pain in my chest. I struggled out of bed, feeling weak. I dressed as fast as I could.

"Eric! Eric!" I pounded on his door loudly. Damien poked his head out from across the hall.

"What's going on?" he demanded as I hammered on Eric's door.

"I need help. I need to get to Everly," I wheezed out, clutching my chest. My neck started to hurt, and I rubbed at it, wincing.

"How can anything be wrong? She's a hell of a lot safer than she's been in a long time. Brighton said he had Marcus Ambrose put wards up to deter the dark creatures."

"Don't. Know," I rasped, now clutching my neck. "Shit. Help me."

Eric's door opened, and he caught me before I fell.

"What's going on?" he asked worriedly. Damien quickly told him what was happening all while tugging his pants and shirt on over his pajamas.

"Get me to her," I huffed, feeling faint. Damien's arm went around me.

"Eric, I'll need your help." Damien called out. Eric disappeared for a moment before returning fully dressed. He got on my other side, and we melded. When we reached Everly's room, Brighton and the two orderlies from the day before were struggling to get it opened.

"Where is *he?*" Brighton shouted, throwing himself against the door.

"I'm here," I called out weakly, coming to him. "What's going on?" I pushed my way forward.

"You don't want to see," the orderly said, his face pale. I pushed him aside and let out a gasp.

Everly was swinging from her bedsheets—her feet inches from the floor, her face pale, and her lips purple.

"Everly!" I shouted her name frantically. "Get out of my way!" I shoved everyone aside and melded. I fell through the door, and my palm came out to catch one of the dead in the forehead. I'd never been able to see them so clearly before. I took out as many as I had to while they struggled to keep me from her. I sent many of them straight to Xanan to be dealt with. Finally, I broke through them and gave Everly's body slack. The door finally banged open, and Damien and Eric rushed in. Within moments, we had her body cut down, and I was holding her, pushing her hair away from her pale face.

"Baby, no," I choked out, cradling her in my arms. "Ever! Come on! Don't leave me!" I sobbed over her barely alive body. "I only just got you," I said softly, pleading with her to come back. I rested my forehead against hers and willed everything I had into that moment. I felt her soul nearby. She was hovering on the cusp of death. I reached forward through the fog and gave her a tremendous tug. She fought me for a moment, but I was so much stronger than she was. I ripped her from the Veil, bringing her slamming back into her body. I felt her draw in a deep breath. And then another.

"Leave us," I murmured. The room emptied in moments. I grew stronger. I felt it as I gazed down at her. This time didn't leave me unconscious. I would've panicked if I hadn't been so grateful to have her back. I laid her down on the floor, melding to a shadow as her eyelids fluttered. I wasn't ready to meet her. I was just Shadow to her.

Her eyes opened, and she gazed up at me.

"Why?" I wept, my chest aching at the thought of losing her. I flickered as I nearly lost control. Quickly, I righted it, feeling heartbroken as I stared down at her. *Why would she do this? Had we broken her so much that she'd been driven to this insanity?* The thought made me sick to my stomach.

Her mouth parted like she wanted to answer me, but nothing came out. Instead, her eyes wavered as she stared up at me. I loosened my hold on her. I leaned down and pressed my mouth to hers, unable to stop myself from finally tasting her sweet lips. She tasted like sunshine. Sugar. She tasted *exactly* how I imagined she'd taste. Her hand cupped my face tenderly. I sighed against her mouth.

"Everly."

I had to go. This was tearing me apart. To know that she would resort to such drastic measures. To know I couldn't be with her in the way I so desperately wanted to. She was alive. She'd be safe now. In my heart, I knew she would be. A lot needed to be done, and I had to make a hard decision. I faded away from her, letting go.

Being without her in my arms was crushing. But I'd see her again. And that was all that mattered.

# CHAPTER 47

*A* week after the incident in Everly's room, I stood in my office staring out the window, dressed in my all black Dementon uniform watching as students milled around, greeting one another after their long summer break.

"Hey, we're leaving," Eric called out, knocking on my door. I turned to him and gestured for him to come in.

"Keep her safe," I said tightly. "The trip here from Rolling Thunder is just over an hour. I'll be timing you. If you're a minute later, I'll come find you."

"Chill," Eric chuckled. "We might stop to get her something to eat."

"Make it quick. She likes her burgers without mayo and onion. She loves pink lemonade. Get it for her and go if she requires it."

"She'll be fine, man. She'll have me and Damien with her. No other student here has *ever* had a Conexus escort."

"I know she's in good hands, but that girl..." my voice trailed off.

"She'll be fine. I promise. I'd die before I let anything happen to her. So would Damien."

"I know." I swallowed hard.

"Why don't you come with us?" Eric asked.

"I can't. I need to stay away from her until she gets adjusted here. I need to maintain my distance. I'm not good for her."

"What are you talking about? You're the Reever. You're *exactly* what she needs."

"I'm not. We're toxic together. We push and pull one another. I need to stay away until things are better sorted."

"What about your rounds to all the new students? Are you going to skip her on your visits?" Eric frowned at me.

"No." I shook my head. "It'll just be really awkward." I went to my desk and yanked a paper out and handed it to him. "You've been assigned as her trainer."

"Man." He sighed and shook his head at me as he took the paper. "Why? We're really doing this?"

"Yes. I trust you with her," I said softly. "You'll do right by her. She needs someone she can trust. You're that guy. You can teach her. I know you can."

"Why don't you? Why are you doing this to yourself? To *her*?"

"I'm just trying to protect her." My lips twitched, torn between tipping up and turning down. "It's best if I go on as if I hate her. I'll only ruin everything if I get involved directly with her."

"You do realize you're making a huge mistake here, right?" Eric asked, studying me.

"I know." I nodded. "But she'll have you. So, it'll be OK."

"I'll take care of her," he said fiercely.

"I don't have any doubts," I replied honestly. "Now go get my mancer. Oh, and let everyone know not to call me Shadow anymore."

"What do you want us to call you then?" Eric frowned at me as he waited for me to speak. I smiled.

"Tell them to call me by my real name. Tell them to call me Raiden."

**To be continued in Grave Secrets, book 3 of The Everlasting Chronicles. . .**

*Enjoy Shadow Song? Please consider leaving your review!*

# ABOUT THE AUTHOR

K.G. Reuss is a *USA Today* bestselling author. She was born and raised in northern Michigan. She currently resides there with her husband, her children, two dogs, a cat, and a few ghosts. K.G. is the author of The Everlasting Chronicles series, Emissary of the Devil series, The Chronicles of Winterset series, and Seven Minutes in Heaven.

When K.G. Reuss isn't pursuing her love for reading and writing, she is working in emergency medicine.

**Come join the street team!**
https://www.facebook.com/groups/streetteamkgreuss

OTHER BOOKS BY K.G. REUSS

*Testimony of the Damned (Emissary of the Devil, book 1)*

*Testimony of the Blessed (Emissary of the Devil, book 2)*

*Gospel of the Fallen (Emissary of the Devil, book 3)*

*Dead Silence (The Everlasting Chronicles, book 1)*

*Shadow Song (The Everlasting Chronicles, book 2)*

*Grave Secrets (The Everlasting Chronicles, book 3)*

*Oracle (The Chronicles of Winterset, book 1)*

*Seven Minutes in Heaven (Single on Valentine's Day, book 1)*

*The Middle Road (K.G. Reuss and C.M. Lally)*

*In Ruins (A Black Falls High Novel)*

# COMING SOON BY K.G. REUSS

*The Dreamweaver Series*
*Rebel Hearts*
*Blindsided*
*Fracture (The Chronicles of Winterset, book 2)*

Printed in Great Britain
by Amazon

56056224R00137